Some women look even better naked than they do clothed, and Michelle was definitely one of them. . . . She had the voluptuous curves of a Rubens woman and the sharp muscle definition of a Michelangelo man. I wondered what I had seen in Sarah's frail, birdlike frame, now that I saw this woman of strong muscle and bountiful flesh.

I didn't have time to admire Michelle for long; within seconds of undressing, she was on top of me . . .

PIECE OF MY HEART

BY

JULIA WATTS

THE NAIAD PRESS, INC.
1998

Printed in the United States of America on acid-free paper
First Edition

Editor: Lila Empson
Cover designer: Bonnie Liss (Phoenix Graphics)
Typesetter: Sandi Stancil

Library of Congress Cataloging-in-Publication Data

Watts, Julia, 1969 –
  Piece of my heart / by Julia /Watts.
    p.   cm.
  ISBN 1-56280-206-2 (pbk.)
  I. Title.
PS3573.A868P5   1998
813'.54—dc21
                                                    97-52960
                                                        CIP

This book is for my friends from the Louisville days, especially Stephanie, Tab, and Keri. As always, my gratitude goes to Carol, Don, Ian, Allison, Dwane, and my mom and dad.

Also, thanks to all of you readers who have attended my signings or written to let me know you enjoy my work. It's always a pleasure to hear from you.

Since in this novel I have attempted to capture the flavor of one of my favorite cities, I have incorporated some real locations into the story. All of the real locations in the novel are use fictitiously, and all of the characters are entirely fictional.

About the Author

A native of southeastern Kentucky, Julia Watts is a part-time teacher, a part-time nanny, and a "rest-of-the-time" writer. She won a generous grant from the Kentucky Foundation for Women for her novel *Phases of the Moon,* which is being taught in a course at the University of Tennessee titled "Images of Women in Literature." Julia holds an M.A. in English from the University of Louisville and is the proud owner of hundreds of books, dozens of fashion accessories, two cats, and five tattoos. Her most recent tattoo is based on Bonnie Liss's gorgeous cover design for *Phases of the Moon.* Julia's fourth novel for Naiad Press, *Wedding Bell Blues,* will be published in 1999.

Books by Julia Watts

Wildwood Flowers

Phases of the Moon

Piece of My Heart

Wedding Bell Blues
(forthcoming)

Chapter 1

It was fall. I could smell it — the old library-book mustiness of decaying leaves, the snap in the air.

Max and Anna were walking ahead of me, holding hands. Their touching made me nervous, afraid some lunatic might be driven to a homicidal rage at the sight of their affection. As it was, all that happened was that some master of the obvious screamed "Dykes!" out of his car window.

"Thank you for noticing!" Max yelled back, but the car was already gone. She turned back to me.

"Get up here, woman. You don't have to walk ten paces behind us, you know."

I scurried up beside them, and Max linked her arm in mine with mock gentlemanly flair. We walked like that, the three of us, arm in arm, not looking like dykes so much as little girls on a playground.

Max and I had gone to college together. She had been one year ahead of me in school and light-years ahead of me in other ways. She seemed to have been out of the closet from the time she was out of the womb — a fact that made the faculty and students at our small-town liberal arts college squirm with discomfort. I'll never forget that day in our French poetry class when tweedy old Professor Oliver suggested that the frequent quarrels between the poets Verlaine and Rimbaud may have stemmed from the fact that they were both deeply in debt.

Max raised her hand. "But, Professor Oliver, don't you think the reason they fought a lot might have been because they were lovers?"

Professor Oliver stared down at his notes through his half-glasses, his bald spot reddening. "Uh . . . well . . . as the New Critics pointed out," he muttered, "perhaps it is unwise to speculate on the private lives of the poets."

Max wouldn't let him off the hook. "Well, I was just curious to know what your opinion was," she went on, "because my high school literature book said that Oscar Wilde was imprisoned because he was deeply in debt, and we all know that's a load of crap. So I guess that whenever I see the phrase *deeply in debt*, I should just mark it out and write in *queer*."

2

She smiled innocently. "Do you think that would be appropriate, Professor Oliver?"

Poor old Oliver just said, "So, in keeping with that New Critical tradition, let's skip the biographical information and look at the poem on page . . ."

The class sat in stunned silence, except for me. I couldn't stop laughing.

I didn't see much of Max outside of class. She was more studious than she let on and spent a lot of time in the library while the rumor mill churned out fictitious romances between her and various female students and faculty members.

As for me, I hung out with what passed for the bohemian crowd. At Hamilton College in tiny Hamilton, Kentucky, being bohemian entailed drinking a lot of beer, having the occasional discussion that revealed your politics to be to the left of Jesse Helms, and making fun of the fraternity/sorority people.

I fulfilled all three bohemian requirements with gusto, and with somewhat less gusto I even maintained a casual heterosexual relationship with one of my compatriots. Since I lacked Max's boldness and had never felt compelled to wear flannel clothing or play fast-pitch softball, I worked with the assumption that I was simply a somewhat underzealous straight girl. Until one night changed everything.

You see, the person I was closest to at Hamilton wasn't my pseudoboyfriend or any of my bohemian beer-drinking pals. It was Sarah.

Sarah and I had been roommates since our freshman year. A small-town girl like me, she'd taken the high road in college, staying in nights and studying for A's while I'd go out drinking and settle for B's. But when I'd finally stagger in at 2:00 A.M. and she'd still be up poring over her chemistry book, we'd sit on my bunk and talk until we couldn't stay awake another minute.

Late one night, just before finals the spring term of our senior year, I came back to our dorm room and was surprised to see that Sarah was not there. Right after I crawled into my bunk, I heard her key in the door. She fumbled a little locking the door, then carelessly kicked off the ballet flats she always color-coordinated with her outfits. I couldn't believe it — she was drunk.

"You asleep, Jess?" she slurred.

"Uh-uh." I propped up on my elbow and looked at her. Her curly blond hair, which she usually pinned back carefully, was loose and wild around her face, and her lipstick was smeared. She looked messy and beautiful. "Looks like you had a festive evening."

"I went up to Richmond with Mike and some friends of his. I figure I've got a four-point-oh, I'm already accepted into med school. What the hell? I might as well get drunk, see what I've been missing the past four years." She unzipped her dress and let it fall to the floor. Wearing just her slip, she tried to climb into the bunk above mine, but fell on her ass, laughing. "Scoot over, Jess," she said finally, "I'm getting in with you."

She slid into the narrow bed beside me, and we fit together like puzzle pieces, my arms wrapping around her, her legs wrapping around me. We started kissing and didn't stop all night long.

When I woke up, my life was transformed. It was like the dreary little house where I had always lived had been blown from gray Kansas to the Technicolor land of Oz.

When Sarah woke up she asked for a glass of water and an aspirin and for us to never speak about what had gone on the night before.

"But . . . didn't you like it?" I asked, my hands shaking as I tried to unscrew the childproof lid from the aspirin bottle.

"That's not the point."

I was trying not to cry. Two minutes earlier I had been happier than I could ever remember being. "So what is the point then?"

"The point is that Mike got accepted into law school at Emory. We're going to get an apartment together in Atlanta. I guess you could say we're sort of engaged to be engaged."

"Oh. I see." Acid tears searing my eyes, I padded down the hall to fetch Sarah's glass of water.

I came to Louisville in part because I knew if I followed Sarah to Atlanta she'd think I was a crazed lesbian stalker and in part because I graduated summa cum lazy from Hamilton, and Louisville State was the only grad school I applied to that offered me a paid teaching assistantship.

After I had set up my futon and bookshelves in the efficiency apartment I found near campus, I was overwhelmed by that disorienting loneliness that comes with moving to a new place. I remembered that Max had moved to Louisville after her graduation, and I found myself looking up her number in the phone book.

Since that initial phone call, I became Max and her girlfriend Anna's designated third wheel. They took me out for art films and Chinese food. They had me over when they had just happened to make so much spaghetti they couldn't possibly eat it all themselves. I was like the old bachelor who gets invited to dinner by the married couple because they worry about his loneliness and poor eating habits.

And so now here we were, arm in arm in arm, browsing through the Saint Mark's Art Fair in the section of town known as Old Louisville. If not for the art fair browsers in their jeans and slogan-bearing T-shirts, you could walk through Old Louisville and believe that you were not living in the twentieth century. The houses were masterpieces of the Victorian era, turreted and towered gingerbreaded mansions with all the dignity and grandeur of a dowager empress decked out in her best lace and jewelry. One house, my favorite, was painted cake-frosting pink with creamy white gingerbread trim. It looked like a candy house, ready to be nibbled like the witch's house in *Hansel and Gretel*.

Dozens of tents were set up throughout the neighborhood, displaying tie-dyed clothes, raku pottery, Japanese silk paintings, African statuary, abstract watercolors, and handmade jewelry. Though it would be a month before I got my first paycheck, I couldn't resist splurging on a small statue of the Venus of Willendorf and a pair of hammered silver earrings.

Max and Anna and I didn't talk much as we toured the fair. We were too busy trying to take in all the sights and smells and sounds and still not bump into strangers. Max did get stopped once by a pair of short-haired women, with whom she chitchatted

6

awkwardly, ending the conversation with an obviously false promise to give them a call sometime.

"Who were they?" Anna asked, when we moved on. Max mumbled something that sounded like "ex-girlfriend."

"Really? Which one?" I asked, eager for gossip.

Max suddenly feigned a great deal of interest in a hideous oil painting. "Um, both of them," she muttered. "Different times, of course."

"Jesus, woman, how many ex-girlfriends do you have in this town?"

Anna studied her nails testily. "I often wonder the same thing."

Max pecked Anna on the cheek. "Oh, don't sulk, hon. Come on, I'll buy you some corn."

"Some corn?" I said. "Now there's a conciliatory gesture. Maybe you wouldn't have so many ex-girlfriends if you could think of something better to ply them with than corn."

"You've never had this corn," Anna said, forgetting her jealousy and gesturing across the street where a black man in a dashiki stood over a huge oil barrel grill. He grilled the corn, husk and all, then peeled it and dipped it in hot, melted butter. The sweet, smoky smell lured us, and soon we were standing in line in front of the grill. "Three, please," Max said when it was our turn, and the man handed us each a steaming, sunshine-yellow ear.

The sweet kernels exploded in my mouth, and the warm butter ran down my chin. I stood with my friends and ate in silence, amazed that something so simple could be so good.

Chapter 2

Dear Sarah,

    I'm writing this at my little cubicle in the English composition office. I've decided that, as a group, graduate teaching assistants are a fairly strange lot (and no, I'm not excluding myself from that pronouncement, thank you very much). You should hear how some of these people talk. Right now, two Ph.D. students are yakking away at the table in the corner, rubbing their little beards thoughtfully and spitting out polysyllabic gobbledygook like "heuristic" and "pedagogical ramifications" and "poststructural thought." I feel like screaming, *This is the* English department, *right? I mean, we* are *supposed to be speaking* English *here?*

Teaching's not bad, though. The little freshmen don't give a good goddamn what poststructural thought means either; they just want to know how to put a paper together that'll get them a decent grade. And since that's something I actually can do, I'm happy to help them with it.

Do you remember Max from school? How could you forget her, right? I've been hanging out a lot with her and her girlfriend, Anna. Anna's nice, but really quiet. Of course, who wouldn't be quiet compared to Max?

So how's med school? Have they let you carve any cadavers yet? And speaking of cadavers, how's Mike? That was uncalled for, I'm sorry. Mike's a nice guy. I just can't help being jealous. I know you think our night together was some kind of drunken abomination, but to me it was a natural extension of our years of talking together, laughing together, living together. I know, I know. I promised not to talk about it, but this is writing, not talking, so I've got you on a technicality.

Sarah, I just want you to know that "je regrette rien," as ol' Edith Piaf would say. And if things between you and Mike don't work out — well, I don't really need to finish that sentence, do I?

I'm sure I've pissed you off by now. Next time I write I'll stick to small talk — nothing more controversial than the weather and fall fashions, I promise. Take care. Be happy.

Love,
Jess

9

As I was folding my letter, Ralph, the part-time instructor whose cubicle was next to mine, poked me on the shoulder. I jumped, but he didn't seem to notice.

"Say, Jess," he began.

Say, Jess was his standard conversational gambit with me. The wiseass in me always wanted to actually say *Jess* in response, but I knew I'd only have to explain it to him. "Yeah?" I said, trying not to be rude but also trying not to show too much interest. It was only my second week in the office, but I had already learned that if I showed too much interest in what Ralph had to say, I'd have to gnaw off a body part to get away from him.

"Say," he repeated, "didja hear that one of Pat Buchanan's relatives was killed at Auschwitz?"

"Really?"

"Yeah, he fell off the guard tower."

I smiled. It was an OK joke, but Ralph had already told it to me twice today. I wondered if the endless cups of coffee and cigarettes he consumed could be contributing to some type of early senility.

"Fell off the guard tower," he hooted. "That's pretty good. Pretty good."

I glanced up at the clock and was grateful to see it was five 'til one. "Well, gotta go teach," I said, grabbing my textbook and turning tail.

"See ya later, Jess," he called, then milking the joke one more time, he added, "Fell off the guard tower!"

Before coming to Louisville State, I had often experienced tiresome political discussions with people whose views differed from mine. The weird thing about Ralph was I agreed with him on almost every issue, but I still found his political discussions tiresome. Perhaps it was because with Ralph, there was no such thing as discussion; he did all the talking, and if you tried to put in your two cents' worth, he'd generally interrupt you.

I always regarded Ralph's wedding band with amazement. Had he actually shut up long enough to let the poor woman say "I do," or had he just pointed at her and said "she will"? When I tried to imagine what kind of spouse would be compatible with Ralph, the only image that would come to mind was a giant ear.

The textbook all the graduate teaching assistants had to use was called *America Singing*. Labeled a multicultural reader, it was designed to help white, middle-class, sheltered college students see things from a less privileged point of view. That day we were discussing an essay by Audre Lorde, whose lesbianism, I noticed (remembering Max's tirade about the closeting of literary figures), was not mentioned in the book's biographical sketch. I decided that at a convenient time, I would mention that Lorde, in addition to being a brilliant poet, essayist, and activist, was also a lesbian.

But as it turned out, there was no convenient time. The discussion became so heated and chaotic that I felt more like a trash TV talk show host than an English teacher.

It all started when the blond-haired, blue-eyed young man in the front row said, "I'm not a racist or anything, but . . . I just found this essay offensive, like the way she wrote *america* and *god* with no capital letters. And I don't know why she was complaining about racism all the time. I mean, slavery was a long time ago."

"Well," I began, trying to maintain a fair and teacherly tone, "certainly it's true that none of us in this room has ever owned or been slaves, but I do think that when you — and I say *you* in the general sense here — that when you live in a society whose economic success has been built on racism, you internalize certain racist values. And while it may seem that slavery was a long time ago, it was only recently that black people and white people couldn't go to the same schools, drink from the same water fountains, or use any of the same public facilities. This is the type of environment in which Lorde grew up." I paused, hoping some of what I said would sink in. "Now let's talk about why Lorde might choose not to use capitalization when she writes words like *god* and *america* —"

A pink-nail-polished hand shot up in the air. "Excuse me, Miss Hamlin?"

"Yes, Amy?"

"I'm just really offended that you said that everybody's racist. I'm not racist at all. Why, if I walk into a room full of people, I don't even notice who's white and who's black."

I didn't even know how to respond to that statement. Why did so many people feel they were supposed to ignore differences instead of accepting them? As it turned out, I didn't have to say anything. The laughter of the two black women sitting in the back of the classroom said it all.

Just as I was trying to think of something to say that might push the white students past their knee-jerk reactions, someone pushed the door open slowly, the way students do when they're late and they think they're being sneaky. In walked a man who, in a classroom full of eighteen-year-olds, looked like a vaguely bohemian chaperone. He was thirty-eight at least, with wire-framed glasses so thick they made him look pop-eyed, shoulder-length dishwater blond hair, and a David Crosby–style mustache. He tiptoed to the head of the class and sat down in an empty chair in the front row. He looked at me and grinned sheepishly. "Grady Combs, ma'am," he said. "Just added your class, ma'am. Real sorry I'm late."

I knew I would have no trouble remembering his name. In the Filofax of my brain, under the heading GRADY COMBS, I engraved the word *hippie*. "That's OK, Grady," I said. "See me after class, and I'll try to catch you up on what you've missed."

The Audre Lorde discussion was so heated that I was exhausted by the end of class. I had heard the phrase *I'm offended* at least ten times. Had I been as naive, as young, as these kids when I was a freshman? Or had growing up in a small town where the few black families literally did live "on the other side of the tracks" made me question the myth that we are in a fully integrated society?

I was all for the multicultural classroom, but I'd be lying if I didn't say I thought about how easy it would be just to lecture about thesis statements and comma splices like my freshman comp teacher had done. People might get annoyed trying to use commas correctly, but they never got offended by talking about them. I had been so busy moderating the discussion that I had completely forgotten to mention that Audre Lorde was a lesbian.

After the room cleared out, Grady came up to my desk. "It seems like it's gonna be a real interesting class, ma'am," he said, seeming a little shell-shocked at having walked in in the middle of such passionate arguing.

"I think so." I was glad to have Grady in class. With his long hair and John Lennon glasses, he would surely bring a much-needed voice of liberalism to class discussions. "Let's see, here's a copy of the syllabus, and here's a card for you to fill out — with your name, phone number, favorite books, movies, music. That way, I'll know a little bit about you."

Grady filled out the card, apologized again for his lateness, and then hurried off to his next class. After he was gone, I glanced down at the card he had handed me. His favorite movie was *It's a Wonderful Life*, and his favorite books were *Think and Grow Rich* and *How to Win Friends and Influence People*. Under the heading marked FAVORITE MUSIC, he had written, "no contest — Neil Diamond." Despite appearances to the contrary, the Summer of Love had apparently passed Grady Combs by. Weird.

On the way back to the office, my eye was caught by a bright pink flyer on the bulletin board.

THE GAY, LESBIAN, AND BISEXUAL STUDENT UNION (GLBSU) MEETS MONDAYS AT 8:00 P.M. IN ROOM 201 OF THE STUDENT ACTIVITIES CENTER

It was quite a change to be at a school with a real gay student group. Max had tried to start a group at Hamilton, but she was the only person who showed up for the meeting. Being in a room full of queers would be a nice break from the company of right-wing students and pedagogy-spewing academic types. My enthusiasm for the meeting was only slightly dimmed by the fact that some master of repartee had scrawled "Die Fags" on the flyer.

I entered Room 201 shyly. "Um, is this the GLBSU meeting?" I felt like an idiot as soon as I asked because the answer was obvious to anybody with a working pair of eyes. There were two hand-holding male couples and one exceptionally lovey-dovey female couple. In the corner, an androgynous young woman sat alone, wearing a T-shirt that read CUNNING LINGUIST.

"It ain't the Society for Creative Anachronism, honey," said a boyish blond man sitting with his older boyfriend. "Have a seat."

I sat down a couple of chairs away from the lesbian couple. I was pretty sure I had seen the long-haired woman in the English department. With her long, flowered hippie skirt and silver dolphin earrings, I figured her for an undergraduate English major, women's studies emphasis.

If I had seen her girlfriend before, I'm sure I would have remembered her. A tiny woman with keen features and spiky strawberry-blond hair, she dressed in the exact way straight people think all lesbians dress: flannel shirt, boots, and Levi's accessorized by the ever-popular wallet and attached chain. But despite having all the trappings of a cliché, the outfit worked on her without a trace of affectation. Just as some women needed to be swathed in silks and satins, she was built for flannel and denim.

"Hey," she turned and said to me. I hoped I hadn't been staring. "I'm B. J., and this," she said, nodding to her partner, "is my wife, Amanda."

"Nice to meet you. I'm Jess." It was the first time I had heard the word *wife* used in a lesbian context. Somehow it made me picture Amanda wearing pearls and high heels and vacuuming while B. J. sat in an easy chair, smoking a pipe and reading a newspaper.

"Haven't I seen you around the English department?" Amanda asked.

"I was going to ask you the same thing, actually. I'm a GTA."

"GTA," B. J. chuckled, "That stand for Great Tits and Ass?"

Amanda elbowed her. "Don't mind her, Jess. She's awful. I'm an undergrad in English, women's studies concentration. I should be graduating in the spring, goddess willing."

Before we could talk more, a shaved-headed, bearded man called the meeting to order. I looked around the room. More people had filtered in, and for the first time I noticed that all the women were sitting on one side of the room and all the men were sitting on the other. This isn't a gay student meeting, I thought. This is a junior-high-school dance.

"Welcome," said the bald, bearded guy. I had noticed the bald-but-bearded look was in among gay men, but the effect always reminded me of Ming the Merciless from *Flash Gordon*. "For those of you who are new here tonight, I'm Alex, the president of the

GLBSU. And tonight Liz, our vice president, will be leading our discussion."

The Cunning Linguist rose from her seat. "OK," she chirped with camp-counselor enthusiasm, "As you can see, I have with me two pieces of poster board and two Magic Markers. I'm gonna give one piece to the guys over here, and then one piece to the women over here." She practically skipped across the room to hand out the poster board. "And what I want each group to do is write at the top of the board: *What I Like Best About Being a Gay Man or a Lesbian*. And then as a group, you can make a list of all the things you like best about being who you are, and then after your posters are done, we'll all get together and discuss them." She smiled brightly.

The results of Liz's little exercise weren't particularly innovative. Topping the men's list of what they liked best was *men*, while *women* topped the women's list. Imagine that.

The whole thing made me kind of uncomfortable. I wasn't much of a joiner, and all group social activities tended to remind me of the few church–youth group meetings I had been forced to attend as an adolescent, where we played stupid and uncomfortably intimate icebreaker games. I still felt embarrassed when I recalled one game in which the object was to transfer an orange from underneath your chin to the same location on another pimply-faced youth without either of you using your hands. The church people probably thought this was a wholesome outlet for horny teenagers' baser instincts.

This poster thing was lame, but it was nothing compared to that little exercise in adolescent

17

humiliation. As long as nobody in the GLBSU asked me to do anything kinky with citrus fruits (in public, anyway) or sing "Kumbaya," I was cool.

After a perfunctory discussion of the posters, Alex said, "Well, if that wraps up our presentation for tonight, I vote that we close the meeting and move our little tea party to the Café Caffeine."

"I second that emotion," said Boyish Blond.

"You wanna go for coffee?" Amanda asked Liz.

"Not tonight — I've got to finish my paper on Noam Chomsky."

Cunning linguist indeed, I thought.

"Hey, Jess," Amanda said, "Are you lesbian or bi?"

I thought for a second. My night with Sarah had certainly transcended my few fumbling experiences with men. "Lesbian," I answered. "Why?"

"Because," Amanda said, "B. J. and I have a tradition of buying a cup of coffee for every new lesbian member of the GLBSU."

"Free coffee with every declaration of lesbianism, huh?" I said. I wondered, if I had been bisexual, would they have bought me half a cup?

Café Caffeine was a standard trendy coffee bar — lots of exposed brick and books lining the walls, so the patrons could feel learned as they sat around getting jittery. My grandfather, an ex–coal miner, has always referred to nursing cups of coffee in public places as *loafing*. With its cinnamon-sprinkled double mocha cappuccinos and cafe lattes and open-mike poetry readings, the Café Caffeine encouraged loafing with pretension.

I sipped my cappuccino and tried to discreetly wipe the foam from my upper lip. Sitting across from Amanda and B. J., I was amused to think I was on

18

my way to achieving third-wheel status in yet another lesbian relationship. "So, how long have you two been together?"

Amanda smiled. "Six months, two weeks, and three days."

"Would you like the hours and the minutes, too?" B. J. added, playing with a strand of Amanda's hair.

"That's OK. I think I get the picture."

"We met in the hospital," Amanda said. "I broke my ankle when I fell out of bed with the woman I was dating at the time. It's a complicated story. Anyhow, I ended up in the emergency room, and B. J. was an orderly there." She glanced at B. J. adoringly. "She took such good care of me, and she looked so cute in her little scrubs, and —"

"And I gave her my phone number."

"And when things with me and the other girlfriend didn't work out —"

B. J. grinned. "We worked out good."

"So." Amanda licked the whipped cream off her spoon. "Are you seeing anybody?"

"No, not really. There was kinda somebody back at college, but she went back to her boyfriend."

"Kinda somebody, huh?" B. J. drained her demitasse. "She sounds kinda straight."

I sighed. "Yeah, but —"

"But she didn't act like it with you, am I right?"

I sighed. "Yep, you're right."

"Well," Amanda said, fishing a lipstick out of her purse. "I'm a firm believer in the idea that there's no such thing as a real straight woman. All women are lesbians. Most of them just aren't lucky enough to have figured it out yet."

That night I stretched out on my futon, trying to

read a particularly dull essay for my history of criticism class. But even as I tried to concentrate on the finer points of literary theory, my mind kept flashing back to what Amanda had said at the Café Caffeine. Was it possible that all women are really lesbians?

It seemed like a bizarre theory. My mom always seemed happy with my dad, and it was impossible to imagine the big-haired sorority girls in college doing the nasty with anybody other than their brainless, frat-boy soul mates. And besides, I sort of liked the idea that being gay made me different from the masses, special somehow.

And yet, if what Amanda said was true, if deep down all women really were lesbians, then might there be just a little speck of hope for Sarah and me?

Chapter 3

"It's kind of embarrassing," Anna said, examining her bandaged hand as we sat on her and Max's front porch, "being attacked by a killer Chihuahua. I mean, I've wrangled Rottweilers, Dobermans...pit bulls, for crying out loud, and then I'm trying to hold this pop-eyed pipsqueak of a dog while Dr. Adams takes its temperature, and the little bastard whips his head around and bites me." She reached over to pet Gertie, her and Max's affectionate but mentally-challenged golden retriever. "You'd never bite me, would you, Gertie?" she baby-talked. "No, Gertie's a good girl."

She scratched the dog behind her ears, and Gertie drooled in ecstasy.

"I may have the ultimate boring office job," Max said, "but at least I don't come home with pieces missing."

I sipped my beer thoughtfully. I had always been awed by Max's intellect when we were at Hamilton, so to me, her current data-entry job seemed like a waste of her talents. "Max, do you ever think about doing something more . . . I don't know . . . meaningful?"

"What? Like getting one of those oh-so-useful graduate degrees in the liberal arts?" She finished off her beer. "Nah, I don't know what I wanna be when I grow up. Right now I just want to take some time for me," she reached for Anna's hand, "and for my sweetie, of course. It was hard at Hamilton, the school being what it was and me being what I was. Now, I just want to take some time to be a dyke."

I smiled. "Is that a full-time job?"

She grinned back and pulled Anna close. "It is if you do it right."

While they kissed, I went into the house to help myself to another beer. Max and Anna's house had a homey feeling which my apartment lacked. There was nothing wrong with my apartment per se — with its futon, bookshelves, and framed Georgia O'Keeffe print. But somehow it looked like the place where I studied and slept, not where I lived.

Though it was just a rented shotgun house, Max and Anna's place seemed both lived in and loved. They had gone to every thrift store in town to pick out furniture, and together they had cleaned it or patched it or painted it until it was more than presentable. Anna had painted the soft, abstract watercolors that hung on the living room and bedroom walls.

Their kitchen was stocked with the stuff of real meals: fresh vegetables and fruit, pasta, rice, oils, and herbs. I thought about the contents of my kitchen cabinets: a half-empty jar of peanut butter and four packages of Ramen noodles. Sure, I envied Max and Anna's passion, but I also envied their domesticity: the everydayness, the permanence of their life together. Standing in their well-stocked kitchen, the thought of having to return to my empty, spartan apartment made me feel unbearably lonely.

Not sure how long I had been lurking inside the house and not wanting Max and Anna to think I was rifling through their belongings, I grabbed three beers from the fridge and headed back to the porch.

"Good God, Jess," Max said, "Just 'cause we were kissing didn't mean you had to disappear for an hour. We weren't gonna do it on the porch or anything."

I felt my face heat up. "Oh, it was nothing like that. It was just time for a potty break. You know what they say, You don't buy beer; you rent it. Speaking of which . . ." I passed the beers around. "Oh, I meant to tell you earlier. Last night at the GLBSU, I met a couple you might know — Amanda and B. J."

Max rolled her eyes. "Yeah, I know 'em."

"B. J. . . ." Anna said. "Omigod, isn't she the one who kept yelling 'Show us your tits' at the k. d. lang concert last year?"

"She's the one," Max said. "If she hadn't been on

the scene long enough to date every dyke in Louisville
— except for me and Anna, I might add — I'd say
she's really a fourteen-year-old boy in dyke drag."

"What about Amanda? Do you know her?"

"I know of her more than I know her. She's also
dated every damn dyke in this town. She used to
have the reputation of being a real crunchy-granola
Birkendyke, but she must be into butch/femme now."

"Isn't Maxie amazing?" Anna said. "Like a walking
lesbian encyclopedia."

Max nudged me on the shoulder. "Did you see
anybody cute last night? That's what those meetings
are for anyway, right?"

"Not necessarily. I mean, student groups serve a
social purpose, but they also have a political
agenda —"

Max laughed a little condescendingly. "Yeah, yeah,
yeah. You're not answering my question."

I thought about the meeting. The only unattached
woman was the too-perky Cunning Linguist, and
though I knew it meant I was probably hopelessly
repressed, I just couldn't see myself going out with
someone who wore a T-shirt like that in public. "No,
I didn't really meet anybody interesting."

"Too bad," Max said.

Anna's eyes lit up suddenly. "Jess, what kind of
things are you attracted to in a woman? I mean, what
kind of women have you dated before?"

"Yeah, fess up, Jess. At Hamilton you were always
hanging out with some slacker guy. I thought you
might be a dyke deep down, but I never had a clue
that you, well, had a clue."

I took a long swallow of beer. "I didn't, for the
longest time. To be honest, I've only ever been with

one woman, and it wasn't like we really dated. It was more like we were friends who drunkenly fell into bed together. I do . . . I did love her, though."

Max was practically salivating at the prospect of such hot gossip. "Was it somebody at Hamilton?"

"Yes."

"Well, go on."

"I don't know if I should tell you who it is or not. I mean, she wasn't exactly thrilled that it happened, and she's living with this guy now —"

"Jess," Max interrupted, "is there any chance that this woman you slept with will be anybody I'll see again at any point in the rest of my life?"

"Well, probably not, but —"

"So tell me. Inquiring minds want to know."

She had me cornered just like she'd cornered Professor Oliver back in our French lit class. "Um, do you remember Sarah Reed?"

Max whooped with laughter. "You slept with Sarah Reed?"

"Not so loud," I said. We were out in the open, after all.

"What's she like?" Anna asked.

Max continued snickering. "Blond hair, blue eyes, Laura Ashley floral-print dresses, pearls her daddy gave her . . . Jess, I'm telling you right now, if that's your type of woman, you're dooming yourself to a lifetime of sexual frustration."

I looked to Anna for sympathy. "It wasn't about what she looked like. It was about the person she was. Smart and much funnier than people gave her credit for being and so . . . gentle."

Anna reached over and squeezed my hand. "You've still got it bad for her, don't you?"

I smiled as much as my grim mood would allow. "Yeah, I guess I do."

"Well, don't worry, Jess," Anna said maternally. "Maxie knows every dyke in this town. She and I are gonna find you a girlfriend."

Chapter 4

Journal Entry: Disaster Date #1

I guess the matchmaking thing was inevitable. Straight or gay, if you play bachelor friend to the nice married couple, sooner or later one of them is going to become possessed by the spirit of Dolly Levy and decide it's time to get you married off. With both Max and Anna working to put an end to my solitary state, I didn't stand a chance.

The date was with the receptionist at the veterinary clinic where Anna worked. Her name was Jennifer,

Anna told me. She was nice, a little shy, and had just broken up with her girlfriend. Max and Anna didn't want to do the double-dating thing; they wanted Jennifer and me to be alone so we could "feel the magic." They even arranged a location for our magical meeting, the Downtown Bistro, a fern bar with alleged ambience. I would know Jennifer because she had long, curly brown hair and would be wearing a blue dress.

I don't know how Max and Anna told Jennifer she could identify me. If they wanted to be accurate, they could have told her I'd be the one biting my nails and breaking out in a cold sweat.

Jennifer was pretty. She had big, doelike brown eyes and the kind of long, wild, curly hair I'd worshiped ever since I saw the cover of Carole King's Tapestry album. Her long, blue dress was printed with tiny moons and stars. She smiled shyly. "Hi."

I smiled back. This wasn't going to be so bad, I thought.

My first mistake was ordering the crab legs. I was chattering away about the weirdness of grad school, trying to be as entertaining as I knew how to be, and Jennifer was grazing away at her salad of baby greens with balsamic vinaigrette.

Then I noticed it. When I cracked open a crab leg, she winced. At first, I wrote her little tic off to nerves and proceeded to dig the meat out of the shell. The second crustacean limb I attacked broke with a deafening "Crack!" and sprayed a fine mist of juice right in Jennifer's face. She swallowed hard and set down her fork.

I was mortified. "Sorry about that," I said, offering her my napkin. "Are you OK?"

"Um, yeah," she said, growing paler by the second. "It's just that the noise bothers me . . . It's like you're sitting across from me breaking this little animal's bones." She hopped up from the table with a quick "excuse me" and made a beeline for the ladies' room.

Needless to say, the knowledge that my date was currently driving the proverbial porcelain bus as a direct result of my grotesque eating habits caused me to lose my appetite. I felt like a disgusting human being. I must have looked like a feasting medieval lord disjointing a chicken, sucking the bones clean, and tossing them over his shoulder to the dogs. When the waiter came back, I asked him to put the rest of my objectionable meal in a doggie bag.

When Jennifer came back to the table, she beat me to apologizing. "I'm really sorry," she said. "I'm a vegan, and I guess I'm just really sensitive about people eating meat. Anna knows about my eating habits, and so I guess I just kind of assumed that since she thought you and I would be a good match, you'd be a vegan, too."

"Um, I don't eat red meat or chicken," I piped up, in a desperate attempt to sound less carnivorous. I didn't eat red meat for health reasons, and I didn't eat chicken because I'd never quite got over seeing my grandmother cut off a chicken's head, only to have its headless body run crazily around her backyard. There was no way I was going to tell that story, though. If the sight of me eating crab legs grossed her out, I'd hate to think what my quaint little Appalachian tale would do to her.

"Well, that's a good start," Jennifer said. "And I don't want you to take this personally, but it's really important to me that the woman I have a relationship *with is as concerned about the rights of animals as I am."*

My first impulse was to act defensive. It wasn't like I had waltzed into the restaurant wearing a mink coat and then proceeded to order veal.

But I held back. The evening was already a disaster. There was no reason to escort my hapless date into a deeper circle of hell. So instead of starting an argument, I limited myself to four words: I understand *and* Check, please.

Office hours are a joke. All GTAs were supposed to keep four office hours per week so that students could come in for one-on-one help with their writing. Like many things in academia, it was a good idea in theory, but the reality was that the last thing on most freshmen's minds is getting one-on-one help with their writing.

I generally used office hours to get my own class work done. Today I was reading an essay on psychological criticism, only to find myself distracted by the puzzling psyches of those around me. Ralph was, thankfully, performing his monologue for ears other than mine. His current audience was a bearded GTA named Tom whose wife sold perfume at a department store to subsidize her husband's study of critical theory.

The only other woman in the office at the moment was Sister Mary Margaret, an ancient nun who came over from the convent two afternoons a week to teach a composition class. She was currently writing the sentence "Please do not write on the blackboard" on the blackboard in perfectly neat, Palmer-technique handwriting. The fact that she was writing a message on the blackboard about not writing on the blackboard did not seem to strike her as ironic. It struck me, of course, but who was I to point out irony to a woman who took orders from a misogynistic man in a dress?

Of course, my own psyche was troubling me more than those around me. Ever since my Saturday night date with Jennifer, I had felt like a disgusting slob, not to mention an oppressor of crustaceans everywhere. It never occurred to me that what you order in a restaurant could be grounds for ending a date. The fact that even the smallest decision could have such consequences made me feel socially paralyzed.

But the crab faux pas was only a minor symptom of what was bothering me. Ever since I moved to the city, it seemed like people were living their lives according to an elaborate set of rules with which I was totally unfamiliar. Hamilton College had given me a good academic education; I was breezing through my classes with no problem. But socially speaking, sometimes I felt as young and naive as the freshmen I taught.

Take the vegan thing. In my hometown of Morgan, Kentucky, if you told someone you were a vegan, they'd say, "I don't believe I've ever heard of Vega. Whereabouts is that?"

Issues like that just don't come up in a small town. My parents are both college educated, but if they know what being a vegan means, it's because they've read about it in a magazine and not because they've ever met one.

That's one of the reasons Sarah and I got along so well. We were both small-town girls who had spent our childhood and teen years with our noses stuck in books. We were operating with a similar frame of reference, and we were comfortable together. I stifled a sigh. It would be nice to feel that comfortable with someone again. If only Sarah would get over this silly, straight-girl thing...

"Excuse me, Miss Hamlin?"

I looked up to face out-of-the-closet Neil Diamond fan Grady Combs, who was dressed in a faded tie-dyed T-shirt and the first pair of Sedgefield jeans I'd seen since the late seventies. "Hello, Grady, have a seat."

"Boy, that must be some interesting stuff you're reading, Miss Hamlin." He grinned and straddled his chair backward. "I thought I'd never get your attention."

"What can I do for you, Grady?"

He knit his brow and scratched his head. "Well, uh, I had some things I wanted to talk to you about ... uh, some things you need to know about me if I'm gonna be in your class."

"Yes?"

"Well, first off, these glasses. I guess you probably already figured out I don't see too good — uh, *well*. Sorry."

I smiled at his self-consciousness. "It's OK, Grady. I turned in my grammar-police badge years ago."

He started laughing, far harder than necessary — a loud, snorting guffaw that lit up his face like a red party-light bulb. He slapped his knee a couple of times, then took off his glasses to wipe the tears that were streaming down his face. A few people had

32

looked up from their desks to see what the deal was. "You sure are a funny lady, Miss Hamlin," he gasped, trying to catch his breath. "But what I was gonna say, though, was I hope you don't mind me sitting in the front row every day, seeing how I'm blind as a bat."

"That's no problem, Grady. And let me know if you ever have a hard time reading my writing on the board."

He grinned. "Oh, you write on the board just fine, Miss Hamlin." But then his voice turned as serious as an anchorman's when delivering the news that the President has just been shot. "The other thing I wanted to talk about was our textbook."

"*America Singing*?"

"Yeah, that's the one. It's a little political, don't you think?"

Uh-oh, I thought, but I turned on my best touchy-feely therapist's and-how-does-that-make-you-feel smile. "How do you mean, Grady?"

"Well, I mean, I don't know about you, but it seems like a bunch of liberal propaganda to me. All these articles by blacks and Indians and lesbians —"

I looked at the picture of Audre Lorde on my desk, hoping I didn't stiffen at the sound of the word *lesbian*. Help me, Audre. "But Grady," I began, "white men are also represented in our text."

"Homosexuals."

I bit my lip, my first instinct being to conk him over the head with my blown-glass paperweight. Calm, I told myself. Breathe. "Now, really," I said, sounding a little more exasperated than I had intended, "Studs Terkel isn't gay. Neither is Ishmael Reed —"

Grady's face was red again, but not from laughter

this time. "That's not my point! My point is, it all comes from one side, you know?"

"You feel your views aren't represented."

This seemed to humor him somewhat. "Yeah."

"Well, Grady, the reason we're using this text is not necessarily to change your political views, but to teach you to think about what you read. You can certainly disagree with the essays, provided, of course, that you read them carefully and give evidence for your opinions."

"So if I disagree with something in the book I can say so in class?"

"Of course." This is going to be a long semester, I thought.

"You know, Miss Hamlin, you're a real understanding person."

"Thank you." Now get out of my office.

"You know, a lot of teachers, they're just so set in their views. It's nice to find one who really wants students to think for themselves. That's what's wrong with this country, not enough people thinking for themselves."

"Well, Grady, I'm glad I could be of help." Whenever someone begins a sentence with the phrase *that's what's wrong with this country*, my policy is to disengage myself as quickly as possible, even if I have to lose a valuable body part in the process. "And if that's all you need —"

"Actually, there is one more thing."

"Yes?"

"I'm studying to be a chiropractor, and I was noticing the other day, your spine curves, doesn't it?"

34

Like a pretzel. Most of the time I don't think about it, but it's still noticeable, even after the back brace I wore through most of high school. "Yes."

"Well, I was just thinking, if you got some orthopedic shoes with about a half-inch lift in the left one, you'd probably have a lot less back pain, and your limp would hardly be recognizable at all." He smiled brightly. "You have a good day now."

He lumbered merrily out of the office. Great, I thought. Assail me with your homophobia, and make me flash back to my adolescent body image problems. The whole hell of it was, he hadn't said the thing about my limp with any trace of meanness. He was actually trying to be nice.

"Jess?"

"Huh?" I flinched, jolted back to reality, and looked up to see Anna standing next to me, with her book bag and portfolio in hand. She worked full-time at the vet clinic and worked part-time on an art degree.

"Who was the hippie you were talking to?"

"That was no hippie."

"OK, whatever. You want to get some lunch?"

I looked at the clock. My office hours had been over five minutes ago. "Sure."

Over salads in the cafeteria, Anna said, "What I want to know is, how was your date Saturday night?"

"I made her puke."

"C'mon, Jess, don't be so hard on yourself."

"I'm not being hard on myself. I literally made her puke." I told her the whole sordid tale. By the time I finished, her head was in her hands.

"Oh, Jess, I'm so sorry."

"You should apologize to Jennifer, not me. She's the one who puked."

"God, I can't believe that. I mean, I knew she was a vegan, but I didn't think it would be that big a deal. I mean, I'm a veggie, and Max is not, but all it means in terms of our relationship is that when we order a pizza, we get one half pepperoni and the other half mushroom."

"Yeah, well," I said, pushing my half-eaten salad away. "Some people take things more seriously than others. Jennifer's a nice person. She just needs to find someone who shares her bunnylike appetites."

Anna smiled and reached over to pat my hand. "I'm sorry the date didn't work out, Jess. Next time Max and I fix you up with somebody, we'll do better. I promise."

Next time. Great.

Chapter 5

Dear Jess,

I got your letter, and I just wanted to write to let you know that Mike and I are officially engaged now. He gave me the ring at this little Italian restaurant near our apartment. He said he knew my daddy was about to have a heart attack, what with the two of us living together without being married, so he wanted to at least make a halfway honest woman out of me. It will be a long engagement, though. We probably won't get married until we both finish school.

The reason I'm telling you all this is so you'll

37

understand why it's so important that we never talk about that night again. Mike just wouldn't understand, and I'm not sure I understand it myself. I still want to be your friend, but only if things can go back to the way they were before. If you can't write me without mentioning that night, then you probably shouldn't write me at all. I had to set fire to the last letter you sent so Mike wouldn't see it.

I guess what I'm trying to say here is that I'm getting on with my life. You should get on with yours, too.

Sarah

After my late lunch with Anna, I had come home to check my mail. When I saw the envelope with Sarah's writing, I bounded up the stairs two at a time, hurriedly unlocked my door, and flopped down on the futon to read it.

Now I lay on the futon, my face buried in a pillow, which muffled my sobs and soaked up my tears. My plan had been to go out later to the GLBSU meeting, but now I knew I couldn't go out. Not now. Not later. Nothing lay beyond my door except more opportunities for pain.

I read the letter over and over again the same way you keep returning to a scab to pick at it, to see if you can make it bleed a little more. Like a true English major, I scrutinized every sentence of her fat, loopy handwriting and asked myself, what did she mean by that?

I still want to be your friend, but only if . . . But only if you erase the most meaningful, most revelatory experience of your life from your memory? *I'm getting on with my life. You should get on with yours, too.* What was I supposed to do — marry some nice, dull-witted boy and then spend the rest of my life pretending to be happy and hetero?

I wrote the words *Dear Sarah* three different times. Each time, tears fell on the paper, smearing the ink, and my mind felt all smeared, too, and I didn't know what to say, so I ripped up the paper and threw it across the room. The pieces scattered, confetti for a cheerless occasion.

It was dark when they knocked at my door. I wiped my swollen eyes and looked at my watch. Somehow it had gotten to be 9:15. I didn't want to answer the door, but the knocking got more and more insistent. Finally, just wanting it to stop, I got up, blew my nose, and unlocked the door to find Amanda and B. J., wearing a lavender dress and a jacket and tie, respectively, in the hall.

"Aha! There she is! We knew you were in there." B. J. eyeballed me for a second and added, "God, you look like shit."

I sniffed pathetically. "That's always nice to hear." I opened the door wider. I didn't feel like having company, but my Southern upbringing didn't allow me to let visitors stand out in the hall.

"We missed you at the meeting," Amanda said, arranging her skirt primly as she settled on the futon, "so we thought we'd stop by and see what was up."

"What are y'all, the GLBSU truant officers? Do I get my dyke membership card taken away now?"

"Aw, it's nothing like that," B. J. said, fiddling with her tie. "Me and Amanda are going down to the Starlite and thought we'd see if you wanted to come, too. Of course, it doesn't look like you're in much of a party mood."

I rubbed my face. I didn't care that I looked terrible. I felt terrible. "What's the Starlite?" I asked, making a minimal effort at conversation.

Amanda and B. J. answered simultaneously, Amanda with "A women's bar," and B. J. with "A dyke bar."

"Well, thanks for the invite, but B. J.'s right; I'm not in a party mood. Maybe some other time."

Amanda knit her brow in concern. "Jess, I know we don't know each other that well yet, but if you need to talk —"

"Talking won't do any good because talking won't change anything." I blinked hard. I couldn't believe there was enough liquid left in my body to produce more tears. "I just got some bad news today, is all."

"Really? What?" B. J. asked.

Amanda elbowed her. "Don't be so nosy. She'll tell us if she wants to."

"It's OK; I don't care who knows. You remember that woman I told you about, the one from college? I got a letter from her today. She's engaged."

"To a man?"

"Yep."

"Bummer." B. J. shook her head. "The straight chicks, man —"

"B. J. —" Amanda chided.

"Sorry. Women, not chicks. Amanda's always trying to raise my consciousness." B. J. stood and hiked up her jeans. "Well, Jess, I think what you need to do here is ask yourself, What would B. J. do in this situation? Do you know what I'd do in this situation, Jess?"

"I'm almost afraid to guess."

"I'd go out and get shit-faced drunk at a beer bust at the Starlite is what I'd do."

"And how would this help the situation?"

"Well, it beats the hell out of sitting alone in a dark apartment. You'd be doing something anyway, and doing something is always better than doing nothing."

"Oh, I don't know . . ." I feared I didn't possess enough will to get myself beyond my apartment door.

"Come on, Jess," Amanda said, "it's not an earth-shattering decision. Just come out and have a beer with us, and if you decide you're too bummed out to be in public, we'll bring you home." She looked me over. "Now go wash your face and comb your hair."

I got up and plodded to the bathroom. My leaden heart made me incapable of taking any initiative, but apparently I could still take orders.

The Starlite was located in a neighborhood of rundown warehouses and seedy taverns across the street from a windowless, concrete-block store that, according to its sign, dealt in XXX ADULT BOOKS VIDEOS NOVELTIES. It wasn't the ideal location for a women's bar, since it was an area where a woman couldn't walk alone without fear of drunken rednecks or trenchcoat-wearing porn store patrons. Or perhaps the Starlite was intended for more fearless women than I.

The bar was easy to miss. Located in a spartan white building similar to the one that housed the adult bookstore, its only identifying label was a small, unlighted sign that read THE STARLITE, with a tiny star dotting the *i*. Apparently, on this end of town, discretion was the better part of staying in business.

B. J. and Amanda joined hands and walked in the door. I followed them, painfully aware of my single state.

Inside, the bar throbbed with activity. A leggy woman in faded Levi's pushed back her mane of blond hair, leaned over the pool table, and began to effortlessly pick off each of her opponent's balls. Near the back of the room, two short, muscular women were engaged in a game of Foosball that was almost erotic in its intensity, while several other women took turns at the dartboard.

The jukebox was blaring a pop song that it was impossible to turn on the radio without hearing lately, and the tiny dance floor was crowded with a double line of dykes, mostly tough butches and fluffy femmes with hardly anyone between those two extremes, swiveling their hips and moving their arms in a choreographed line dance. A couple of the women hip-swiveled with unbearably sexy abandon. Most of them, though, looked uncomfortable performing such a private motion in public and were too busy counting out their steps to worry about their level of finesse.

Except for a few necking couples, nobody in the bar was sitting down; everybody was doing something. Between the pool and the darts and the Foosball and the dancing, I felt like I must be the most sedentary, uncoordinated dyke who ever lived.

When we went up to order our drinks, the bartender, a stout woman in her thirties, looked at me and said, "I don't believe I've seen you here before."

"Nope, this is my first time."

"Well, we'll be gentle with you then." She winked. "I'm Stella. I own the place."

"Stella by Starlite, huh?" I said. "Well, it's a nice place."

She handed me a plastic cup of draft beer. "You're a college girl, ain't you?"

"Yeah, I guess I am."

"Well, you be sure to tell your school friends about this place, you hear?"

"I'll do that." The thought of having "school friends" made me feel about twelve years old. I looked at the signs that adorned the barroom's hot-pink walls: WED NITES 6–9, ALL U CAN EAT BBQ RIBS and THURSDAY NITES DON'T MISS OUR LADY VENUS EXOTIC DANCERS REVUE. I thought about the crab-leg incident and wondered how Jennifer would react to a barroom full of dykes gnawing on charred pig flesh. Between the ribs and the strippers, the women at the Starlite weren't accumulating many political correctness points, but they did seem to be having an awfully good time.

"You want to sit down?" Amanda asked.

"Is that allowed here," I asked, "or are we required to participate in some physical activity?"

"I'm saving up my energy for the physical activities later tonight," B. J. said, giving Amanda a squeeze.

"Oh, stop," Amanda giggled, but she clearly didn't mean it. Some women might have found B. J.'s endless innuendos tiresome, but she loved the attention.

"Hey, y'all." A woman leaned heavily on our table.

Dressed in jeans and a denim workshirt, she held a flamingo-pink cocktail that looked like it would've been more at home in the hand of a drag queen.

"Hey, Sal," B. J. hollered over the blaring jukebox. "What the hell are you drinking?"

"Aah, it's called a pink pony or a pink squirrel or some kinda shit like that. It was on special, so I figured I give it a try. It tastes like Kool-Aid and cough syrup, but hey, a drink's a drink, right?"

"How's Carly?" Amanda asked.

Sal shrugged and drained half her drink. "I wouldn't know. She dumped me last week. I've been through four girlfriends in ten months. That's a shitty record, even for me."

"I'm sorry to hear that, Sal."

"Yeah, it sucks." She fished a Marlboro out of her shirt pocket. "You know, she actually had the nerve to tell me she was leaving because I have a drinking problem." She lit her cigarette and exhaled a cloud of smoke. "Drinking problem, my ass. Like the T-shirt says, I get drunk, I fall down — no problem. Besides, she can't fool me. I know she's been stepping out with that drag king that works over at the Jiffy Lube."

Amanda nodded in my direction. "Jess here just got some bad news, too."

Sal eyed me with interest, ready to form a bond based on our mutual heartbreak. "Oh yeah? What's that?"

"My dog back home just died," I lied. I could see the matchmaking wheels in Amanda's mind turning. There was no way I was going to become the next brief episode in Sal's ongoing soap opera of serial monogamy. Besides, if I had wanted drunken, sloppy sex, I would've stayed straight.

"Aw, that's too bad. Let's drink a toast to ol' Rover." We raised our glasses in tribute to my nonexistent deceased dog, then Sal's eyes strayed just as I had hoped they would. "Hey, B. J.," she stage-whispered. "You see that girl in the red dress over in the corner?"

"Yeah, I see her."

She ground out her cigarette. "I'm gonna make her mine."

"Not without getting the shit beat out of you," B. J. said. "She's Pam's girl."

Sal drained her drink, full of bravado. "Not for long, she ain't."

"I'm warning you, Sal," B. J. said, "You're gonna get your ass kicked."

"Hey, I figure I'll either get laid or get my ass kicked. Either way, something interesting happens, am I right?" She smoothed out her shirt and adjusted her collar. "I'm gonna go talk to that girl. I'll catch you gals later."

After Sal left, Amanda said, "Jess, why did you lie to her like that?"

"I'm just not the kind of person who likes to tell the world my troubles."

"I just thought the two of you could — you know, comfort each other."

"No offense, Amanda, but adding Sal's problems, which appear numerous, to my own is hardly a recipe for comfort. Disaster, yes. Comfort, no."

"Sal means well," Amanda insisted. "She just needs somebody to look after her, make sure she doesn't drink too much."

I was growing impatient. "Well, Carrie Nation I ain't. I'm not in the business of saving anyone from herself or from demon rum. I have a hard enough time holding my own shit together."

"You might as well give up, Amanda," B. J. said. "Jess isn't about to drop that torch she's carrying for that straight girl."

"It's not just about Sarah," I said, sounding shrill despite my efforts to the contrary. "It's also that I don't want to hook up with some random woman just because I'm hurting right now."

"All we're trying to do," Amanda said, "is get you away from the straight women. Trust me, Jess. You've not been with a woman until you've been with a real, live lesbian. It's —"

"What she's trying to say," B. J. interrupted, "is you've not been with a woman 'til you've been with me."

"You're not making her an offer, are you, hon?" Amanda's tone was teasing, but I detected an undercurrent of jealousy.

"Of course not, baby." B. J. wrapped her arms around her girlfriend. "I just wanted to let her know what she's missing." She leaned into Amanda for a kiss.

I waited for them to come up for air. They didn't. Finally, I swallowed my last mouthful of tepid, diluted draft beer and decided it was time to wander up to the bar for a refill.

To be honest, Amanda and B. J. were getting on

my nerves. Here I was, trying to get my mind off this woman, and they bring me to a lesbian bar where they talk about nothing but lesbians and lesbian sex. It was like they were forcing me to think about the one thing I didn't want to think about — as though I had said, "Look the only thing I don't want to think about or talk about is hippopotamuses" and so to distract me, they took me to the zoo.

At the bar, I handed my plastic cup to Stella. The fact that they served the body-temperature yellow liquid in plastic cups made it bear a disquieting resemblance to a urine sample. I glanced back at my table. Amanda and B. J. were still locked in a clench.

"Let me guess. Third wheel, right?"

I turned around to face a black woman who was at least a head taller than I am. Her hair was in long, thick braids, and a gold ring sparkled in her nose. "Excuse me?" I said.

"I like to guess things about people. And I was just guessing that you came here with those two girls who are practically doing the wild thing on that table over there, and now you've got nothing better to do than drink this piss-water they serve for beer here."

I smiled. "You must be psychic."

"No, I just notice things. See those two?" She gestured to another necking couple behind the pool table. "I came with them."

I laughed. "After a few beers, a couple's interest in making small talk does tend to flag, doesn't it?"

"Tell me about it." Her liquid brown eyes sparkled with good humor. "You been here before?"

"Nope."

"Me neither. The thing is, Lynn — that's my friend

from work who's got her lips Krazy Glued to that blonde over there — she told me this place was really, how did she put it? Mixed." She surveyed the room. "Mixed? Hello! This place is about as racially diverse as a Daughters of the Confederacy meeting. That's the thing about having white friends; they just don't notice these things. They see one black person in a place once, even if she's mopping the floor, and boom! It's a center of multicultural activity."

I didn't know what to say, so I smiled and sipped my beer.

"Hey, don't look so nervous. I just needed to vent for a minute. I'm back to being my even-tempered self now." She held out her hand. "I'm Michelle, by the way."

Her handshake was firm, but not the bone-crushing grip of someone who's trying to impress you. "Jess."

"So, Jess, what do you do in real life?"

"In real life?"

"You know, when you're not hanging out in dyke bars — when you're among Them instead of Us."

"Oh. I'm a grad student over at the university — in English."

"English, huh? I majored in theater over at Frankfort State. I like the technical stuff — lighting, sets, that kind of thing. I moved here after graduation because there're lots of theaters here and because I was too chickenshit to move to New York and starve with all the other bohemians. As far as I'm concerned, there's nothing glamorous about starving for your art."

"Have you found some theater work here?"

"I've got plenty of work with little theater companies. Trouble is, I don't get paid a red cent. So my real life is theater work, and to pay the rent I work at APD like every other dyke in this city."

"APD?"

"Girl, you've not lived here long, have you? APD — American Parcel Delivery. It's a bunch of dykes in baby-shit-brown polyester uniforms lifting heavy packages over their heads and loading them onto trucks. It's a boring as hell job, but it gives you great biceps." She rolled up the sleeve of her T-shirt and flexed her arm. "Feel."

I lifted up my hand and hesitated, shy suddenly.

"What's the matter? You never touched a black person before? Don't worry; it's not catching."

I laughed, but deep down I was uncomfortable because I realized I never had touched a black person before. How strange. I squeezed the hard knot of muscle. "Wow." It really was impressive. Sarah's body had been soft right down to her tiny bones — fragile and delicate, almost birdlike. But underneath Michelle's soft skin there were strength and resilience.

After I drew my hand away, we stood in silence. "So," I said, trying to milk humor out of the awkwardness, "I guess this is one of those pauses when we search frantically for a suitable topic of conversation."

Michelle looked me directly in the eye. "Do you have a girlfriend, Jess?"

I looked at my beer cup, my shoes, anything to keep from meeting her gaze. It had been fine when it was just a friendly conversation, but my touching her had changed things. "Um, yeah," I heard myself saying.

"Where is she tonight?" I thought she sounded suspicious, but maybe it was just my imagination.

"Uh, she's in Atlanta, actually. At Emory med school. I was going to go to grad school at Emory, but my grades weren't high enough. So right now, we have kind of a long-distance relationship."

"That must be rough."

"It is." I felt terrible lying to her, but lying felt like my only option. I couldn't just start spilling my guts about Sarah; she'd think I was pathetic. And besides, there was always the chance that when I'd finished my tale of woe, she'd say, "Well, why don't you go out with me then?" And I'd say ... what? I'd have to say no. I couldn't open myself up to a woman again just so she could find my most vulnerable places.

"Jess, are you OK?" Michelle looked worried; I must've been visibly freaking out.

"Yeah, sorry. I guess I got to thinking about Sarah."

"Well, I just wanted to make sure you weren't tripping out on my account. I'm not a mad stalker or anything. I was just liking talking to you and I figured it never hurts to ask, right?"

"No, I guess not."

"Excuse us for interrupting." I looked up to see Amanda, who was leaning so close into B. J. that they looked like Siamese twins. "We were about to leave and wondered if you still wanted a ride or if" — she cast her eyes toward Michelle — "you were taken care of."

"I still need a ride," I said, too quickly. "Um, nice talking to you, Michelle."

"Hey, wait a minute." Michelle grabbed a business card off the bar, scribbled something on it, and handed it to me. "Give me a call sometime if you want to. We can just, you know, hang out."

I shoved the card into the pocket of my denim jacket. "OK, well, see ya."

After we got in the car, B. J. said, "Jess, I don't know why you're letting us take you home."

"Me neither," Amanda chimed in. "That woman was hot!"

"Look, y'all. I'm just not into the casual sex thing, OK? Not that she offered."

"Woman, she was offerin' all over the place!" B. J. yelled, hitting the dashboard for emphasis. "A little nooky would've been just the thing to get your mind off what's her name, make you realize she's not the only woman in the world with a working tongue and fingers!"

Amanda laughed. "Besides, Jess, there aren't many black dykes in this town, not out ones anyway. And black women are sooo beautiful." She paused reflectively. "Do you know that I've never been with a black woman? I've been with an Asian woman, an Italian woman, a few older women, one legally blind woman — but never a black woman, just because the opportunity has never presented itself. And tonight you had the opportunity, and you passed it up. I don't believe it!"

I wasn't sure I liked Amanda's attitude. "I didn't know I was supposed to keep a scorecard. If I sleep with all the types of women on the list, do I earn a special lesbian merit badge?"

"It's not like that." Amanda sounded irritated. "It's just that I think you should keep yourself open to new experiences."

I was all for new experiences, too, at least in theory. But I was uncomfortable with the way Amanda seemed to look at sleeping with women of different ages, physical types, or ethnic groups in the same way someone might regard sampling different exotic dishes in foreign restaurants. It seemed to dehumanize the sex partner, to turn her into an exotic piece of meat — into Peking duck or lamb vindaloo instead of a full-fledged person.

"Well, if I had chosen to go to bed with Michelle," I said, "assuming it was even an option, I would've done it because she is Michelle, not because she is black."

"You know what your problem is, Jess?" B. J. said, pulling in front of my apartment building.

"What?" I figured she was going to tell me whether I wanted to know or not.

"You're a hopeless romantic."

"You're probably right." I opened the car door. "Well, g'night. Thanks for taking me out."

When I turned on the light in my apartment, I saw Sarah's letter on the living room floor, right where I had left it. I picked it up and read it again. The pain shot back through me, just as fresh and sharp as it had been this afternoon. I put the letter down and sighed. A hopeless romantic — that's what I was, all right — with emphasis on the *hopeless*.

Chapter 6

Dear Sarah,
   I'm sorry you feel the way you do. If you ever change your mind . . .

A beefy hand shook my shoulder. "Say, Jess?"

I looked up from my desk to see Ralph's beady eyes staring at me. "Didja hear this one? How many fundamentalists does it take to screw in a lightbulb?"

I shoved my letter to Sarah under a pile of student journals. "I don't know, Ralph. How many?"

"Three. One to screw in the new lightbulb, one to pray for the old lightbulb's soul, and one to say that screwing's a sin."

I grinned. "That's pretty good."

I hoped my comment would curtail his obligatory repetition of the punch line, but he still slapped his desk and hooted, "Screwing's a sin!"

I smiled weakly, opened a student's journal, and began to feign an enormous amount of interest in it. It's amazing what students will write in their journals just to fill the required number of pages. The entry I was scanning in order to avoid Ralph was one student's excruciatingly detailed account of her routine visit to the gynecologist. Great, I thought. The last thing I want to do while I'm lecturing on comma splices is picture one of the students in the front row with her feet in stirrups. The last sentence of the entry was, "And finally, the doctor put his finger in my anus." Not knowing what kind of teacherly comments to write at the end of such a personal account, I scribbled, "Why are you telling me this?"

At 3:00 I went upstairs to meet with Dr. Graham, my faculty mentor. Dr. Graham's office was a tribute to women in literature. The walls were so covered with posters and picture postcards of female authors that not one inch of institutional concrete peeked through. I surveyed the intelligent faces — Edna St. Vincent Millay, Zora Neale Hurston, H. D., Gertrude Stein — and felt I was in very good company.

Dr. Graham was good company, too. Her bright, alert eyes made her look right at home among her literary foremothers. She poured coffee into a mug decorated with a caricature of Emily Dickinson. "What's the verdict, Jessica?" she asked.

"The verdict on what?" Dr. Graham was the only person I allowed to call me "Jessica," probably because I liked the sound of the extra syllables coming from her lips. Ever since Miss Becky, my raven-haired student teacher in the first grade, I had had a tendency to get dewy-eyed, hero-worship crushes on smart, attractive female teachers. Of course, there weren't many crushworthy faculty members at Hamilton, since they tended to be either of the tweedy male or grandmotherly female variety.

"The verdict on teaching, first of all."

"I like to teach, hate to grade."

She smiled knowingly. "Everybody hates to grade. If you said you liked it, I would've worried about your sanity." She sipped her coffee. "Let's see . . . you're taking introduction to scholarship and history of criticism, right? How are those going?"

"I'm doing fine in both classes, but neither of them is exactly riveting. I'd rather be digging into some real literature instead of just talking about it."

"Those classes aren't supposed to be riveting. That's why they're required. The department makes all entering grad students take those two classes in hopes that they'll get bored and go home."

The creases in the corners of her eyes told me she was joking. I let myself laugh.

"Are you getting along OK otherwise — making friends and all that?"

"I have a few people in my life to tempt me away from my studies."

"That's good. A lot of people are lonely their first year at grad school." She paused for another sip of coffee. "Let's see, Jessica . . . did you tell me you're engaged?"

"No," I said with more emphasis than was necessary.

"Hmm. It must have been one of the other new students, then." "Must've been." I couldn't help feeling a little hurt that she couldn't distinguish me from the other female grad students. Just like in grade school, I wanted to be the teacher's pet.

"I'm glad you're not engaged, Jessica. Too many young women fall in love and let their personal lives interfere with their careers."

I don't know why I said it. Maybe it was the face of Gertrude Stein staring at me expectantly from the wall, but all of a sudden, I heard myself announcing, "I'm gay, actually."

She didn't bat an eye. "Well, no need to worry about marriage keeping you out of a good Ph.D. program, then. I think Duke or Virginia for you. As I recall, your undergraduate grades could be better, but if you do well here and maybe publish a paper or two, you might be able to get in."

I don't know what kind of reaction I was expecting. Maybe, "I'm gay, too — welcome to the fold, sister" or at least "How nice for you." At any rate, I hadn't expected her response to be quite so . . . academic.

Made uncomfortable by my silence, she finally said, "I like men myself. I guess you couldn't tell it by looking at my office, though, could you?" She giggled nervously in Gertrude Stein's direction. "As a matter of fact, I think you know my husband."

I scanned my memory. "I don't think so."

"Oh, you know him; you just didn't know he was my husband. We don't really broadcast our relationship. He's a part-time lecturer in the department. His desk is right next to yours in the comp office."

"Ralph?" I hoped my voice didn't convey the magnitude of my shock, but I feared that it did.

She smiled self-consciously. "I don't know why people always act so surprised when I tell them that."

I looked at Dr. Graham's pretty round face and dark, wavy hair and pictured her sharing a bed with Ralph — Ralph with his incessantly moving lips and beady eyes and nicotine-yellow fingers. It wasn't just the matter of looks, though; it was that Ralph was so annoying. I tried to smile normally. "Well, opposites attract, I guess."

Later that day, when I taught an essay on gender roles in comp class, Grady Combs said he thought that it was a woman's duty to her husband to look pretty and feminine at all times. Between Grady's piggishness and the news that Dr. Graham and Ralph were united in the eyes of God and the state, I was getting a tremendous headache. Heterosexuals, I thought. Go figure.

Dear Jessie,

Just thought I'd drop you a note to let you know we're thinking of you. It's hard to get used to you being so far from home. I know Louisville is just a couple of hours up the interstate from Hamilton, but you being in the city makes you feel farther away somehow. I feel sorry for mamas whose kids live on the other side of the country, since I'm having a hard time with you just living on the other side of the state!

Things in Morgan are going along about like usual. No big surprise there. My job's the same as ever — typing, filing, and fetching. But your dad insists he's got the unruliest bunch of eighth-graders he's ever tried to teach. Of course, he says that every year.

Your nanny and papaw are doing as well as can be expected. Papaw needs the oxygen machine to breathe most of the time, and Nanny's mind's not getting any better. We did hire a new woman to stay with them though, and she's good at making sure Papaw takes his medicine and Nanny doesn't burn the house down. It's hard to watch your parents get old.

Did I tell you that Tracy Davis (her married name's Holcomb) just had her third baby? It's a boy, and she named him Joshua Noah or Noah Joshua, I don't remember which. She's just twenty-two and already has three babies. It won't be long 'til that skinny little cheerleader's body she was always so proud of starts spreading and sagging. Anyway, I thought you might like to know that Morgan High School's most popular girl has turned into a regular baby factory.

Well, I'd better sign off for now. Your dad and I miss you. Study hard, but rest, too. We can't wait to see you at Thanksgiving and catch up on what's going on with you.

Love
Mom

I knew I had never been built for life in Morgan, Kentucky. Things progressed so simply there: birth, growth, school, marriage, reproduction, aging, death. Some part of me envied Tracy Davis and wished I could be a happy little wife and mother who carries a covered-dish casserole to the Morgan First Baptist Church every Wednesday night and feels certain that God is in his heaven and all is right with the world. I wondered what it would feel like to be certain of something, of anything.

Thanksgiving was only a little over a month away. I wanted to go home and see Nanny and Papaw on what might be their last Thanksgiving. And I wanted to see Mom and Dad, too, but my stomach knotted at the thought of spending time with them because they wanted to know what was going on with me, and the one thing I was certain of was that I didn't have the guts to tell them.

Chapter 7

"A toast," the aging female impersonator proclaimed, holding her shot glass aloft in scarlet talons:

"A young man by the name of Gene
Loved the British royal family scene,
So aiming to please,
I bowed down on my knees
'Til he cried out, 'God save the queen!' "

She drained her drink, leaving a crimson lipstick

smudge on her glass. "Welcome to Expressions. I'm your hostess, Faith Hope Charity, telling you to drink up, dance up, and smoke 'em if you've got 'em!"

She pushed a tendril of her not-to-be-found-in-nature red hair out of her kohled eyes and peered backstage. "You ready back there, honey?" she called to someone in the wings. "You got your tits on?" She laughed. "OK, then." In that case, the cast of Cherchez La Femme is proud to present the Southeastern sex bomb, Miss Sugar Cane!"

Faith Hope Charity skittered offstage, and a gorgeous bottle-blonde slithered on wearing a fringed red gown that showed off some stunningly realistic curves. She began to coquettishly lip-synch to "Diamonds Are a Girl's Best Friend" — the Marilyn version, of course. "Wow," I whispered to Max and Anna.

Max leaned over the table. "Don't be too impressed. She's had the chop."

"The what?"

"She's had a sex change," Max explained. "She totally lives as a woman now. Some people think she shouldn't be allowed to perform anymore, since she's not exactly impersonating a female."

"That's what Faith's little got-your-tits-on barb was about," Anna added. "It was a little dig at Sugar. Faith knows damn well that Sugar's got her tits on — they're bought, paid for, and permanently attached."

I looked up at Sugar as she shimmied around on stage. She certainly got what she paid for.

"And since Sugar is now a woman who dates men, she considers herself straight. She's always gone in for the macho frat-boy type anyway." Max looked up at the stage. "Watch her."

A muscular young man who looked like he could be president of the Student Republicans stood in front of the stage, holding a dollar bill. Sugar dipped gracefully, tucked the dollar into her cleavage, and rewarded the young man with a kiss so lengthy that it caused some of the song lyrics to go un-lip-synched. When an older, heavier, more obviously gay man offered her a dollar, she handled it as though it were a dead rat, and walked away without giving him so much as a peck on the cheek.

"That was cold," I said, sipping my watery gin and tonic. "I hope people who have sex changes aren't always like that."

"Oh, hell, no," Max said. "Most people come out of the experience queerer than ever. Miss Junior League Wanna-be up there is just an unfortunate exception to the rule."

Our trip to Expressions was certainly proving educational. I had never been to a big gay bar with a drag show before, and Expressions' Cherchez La Femme troupe was one of the finest collections of drag queens in the Southeast.

The club was almost overwhelmingly big. The cabaret where we sat consisted of three tiers of tables — the kind with tablecloths and little lamps like in nightclub scenes in old movies — facing a large stage with a glittering silver curtain. And this was only one room of the bar; we hadn't even been to the disco yet. It was quite a contrast from the seedy-but-homey Starlite, both in ambience and clientele.

As I scanned the room, I noticed very few women. Nattily dressed young men sat in pairs or in groups. Sometimes a woman would be sitting with a group of men, but she was invariably heavily made-up with overprocessed hair, in all likelihood not a sister, but a straight female friend or coworker who thought it might be fun to see a "real gay bar."

The only female couple I saw, other than Max and Anna, sat in a dimly-lit corner and looked as though they might be visiting from one of the small Kentucky or Indiana towns surrounding Louisville, so awed did they seem by Expressions' size and opulence. Of course, I was awed, too, and I probably looked as out of place as they did.

The show went on. Faith Hope Charity did a campy Tammy Wynette medley, starting with "Stand by Your Man" and ending with "Your Good Girl's Gonna Go Bad." A statuesque black queen lip-synched a love ballad by a closet-case pop diva, and then a voice over the intercom boomed, "Ladies and gentlemen, the cast of Cherchez La Femme is proud to present the fastest thing in Louisville this side of Churchill Downs — Miss Rickie Lee!"

"Oh, God help us," Anna said.

"What do you mean?"

"Just wait."

The lights came up on a middle-aged blonde in a hot-pink cocktail dress. She lip-synched her way through a Dusty Springfield number, then turned on the mike. "Yo, bitches!" she hollered in a husky voice that made her sound like my bleached-blond, chain-smoking Aunt Betty. Come to think of it, she didn't look unlike Aunt Betty. "Now wait a damn minute here. When I say 'yo, bitches,' you should at least have the decency to yell 'Yo, bitch!' back at me. Let's try it again." She took a breath, then yelled, "Yo, bitches!"

"Yo, bitch!" a chorus of voices called.

"Interrrressting you should call me that," she purred, stepping down off the stage. "I must be about to get my period or something, 'cause, honey, I am a *bitch* tonight!"

Several people laughed and applauded.

"Now, let's see, who all's here for the first time tonight?"

I raised my hand until Max elbowed me in the ribs and hissed, "Put it down!"

It was too late; Ricki was already hovering over our table. "Now what do we have here . . ." she purred, clicking her hot-pink nails. "We have a pair of lezz-bee-uns and . . ." She made an elaborate show of sniffing the air, then peered down at me like a brightly colored bird of prey. "I smell . . . straight pussy!" She put on a mock psychiatrist attitude. "So tell me, madam, how long have you been a het-er-oh-sex-yoo-al?"

The mike was in my face, and all I could do was stutter, "I, uh . . . I'm . . ." But before I could form an answer in my head, let alone get one out of my mouth, Anna leaned over the table and planted a big, showy kiss on my mouth.

"Well, I guess I'm losing my touch — or my smell," Ricki said, dabbing delicately at her nose. "David, get these girls another round of whatever they're having." And after making that conciliatory gesture, she flitted off to find her next victim.

"Anna, I can't believe you did that!" I laughed.

"No kidding," Max said. "You're usually Miss Prim and Proper, compared to me anyway."

"But that's not saying much." Anna sipped her

free drink, then glanced nervously at Max. "You're not mad at me, are you?"

"What for?"

"For kissing Jess."

I looked down into my drink, suddenly feeling like I wasn't in the room.

"There's no reason for me to be mad. You just did it to get Jess out of an uncomfortable situation, right? And besides, I can't be jealous of y'all. What kind of sexual chemistry could you two girlie-girls scrape up?"

"We are not girlie-girls!" Anna protested.

Max rolled her eyes. "Hon, do you know what the contents of my bathroom were before you moved in? A bar of soap, a bottle of shampoo, a toothbrush, and a tube of toothpaste. And now every available inch of bathroom space is crowded with cruelty-free apricot facial scrubs and hyacinth hair conditioners and peppermint foot lotions and bergamot bath oil beads. Now I don't even know what half that shit's for, but I know somebody who considers it all one hundred-percent necessary to her daily existence."

"Well, what about me?" I asked. "How am I a girlie-girl?"

"That's easy," Max said. "Look at your accessories. You've got your little silver kitty-cat brooch on your blazer to match your little silver kitty-cat earrings. Also . . ." She leaned toward me and squinted, "You're wearing nail polish on your toes, aren't you?"

"How did you know that?"

"Elementary, my dear Hamlin. I've seen the stupefyingly huge nail-polish collection you keep in your bathroom cabinet. I was confused by it at first because I'd never seen you with polished fingernails. Then I started noticing when you were walking around barefoot: Your toenails are always painted."

"I just think feet need a little extra help to be aesthetically pleasing. Hey, wait! You snooped around in my bathroom cabinets?"

Max shrugged. "Hey, su casa es mi casa. Besides, can you honestly say you've never looked through another person's stuff before?"

I thought back to my babysitting days in high school. After the kids were asleep, I'd always look in the parents' bedroom drawers in hope of finding interesting sexual devices. I was always disappointed. "Sure, I've gone through people's things before. I've just never had the nerve to tell them about it."

"That's my Maxie," Anna laughed. "She can't keep a secret, even about herself."

"So you're saying that two very feminine women can't have a mutual sexual attraction?" I pressed.

"I'm not saying they can't. I'm just saying that in my experience, they usually don't." Max finished off her beer. "Besides, it's hard for two girlie-girls to settle down together. Where would they find room for all their damn toiletries?"

I smiled, then asked softly, "What about Sarah and me?"

"That," said Max, "is one of life's greatest mysteries. Besides, you two haven't exactly settled down together, have you?"

She was only stating the obvious, but I still felt as though she'd punched me in the stomach.

"Hey, I know," said Anna, cushioning the blow. "Why don't we go dance?"

"Yeah, OK," Max said, then touched my shoulder. "I'm sorry, OK?"

"No need to be sorry. You didn't say anything but the truth."

As it turned out, we couldn't dance because at the disco, it was Country-and-Western Night. Pairs of men, all dressed like the cowboy guy in the Village People, were do-si-doing and buck-and-winging and generally doing whatever it is that country-and-western dancers do. Since we were clueless about the steps, we stood and watched for a while. A fast number came on, and Busby Berkeley suddenly met *Urban Cowboy* as the men automatically fell into single-file lines and started doing an elaborate series of stomping steps.

Line dancing was a great hobby for gay men, I decided. Depending on your proclivities, you could pretend you were a cowboy or one of the Radio City Music Hall Rockettes. I was enjoying watching, but soon Max indicated that it was time to leave the homo hoedown.

"I can't listen to country music too long," she explained. "It reminds me of my upbringing. Let's go to the front bar. They've got a pinball machine."

We walked out of the disco and past the flower-and-card shop to the front bar. Except for a few people sitting on barstools, the room was mostly empty. On small platforms against the walls, tan, shirtless, go-go boys shook their booties for no one in particular. We made our way to the pinball machine.

Suddenly I felt a hand on my shoulder. I turned around to face one of the bearded GTAs from the English comp office.

He smiled. "Jess, right?"

"Yeah." I fished desperately for his name. "Christopher?"

"That's me. I've seen you around the office, but I never had a clue you might be, you know . . ."

"It's because she's a girlie-girl," Max piped up.

"Shut up, Max," I laughed. "Well, I didn't have a clue about you either." If I had really thought about him individually and not just lumped him in with all the other bearded GTAs, I probably would've figured it out. Straight guys named Christopher always wanted you to call them Chris.

"Well, maybe we should get together for coffee sometime," he said. "Now that we know we have more in common than just being nerdy English grad students. The GTAs are a surprisingly straight lot, don't you think?"

"Oh, yeah. We token queers definitely need to stick together." I asked him if he was familiar with the GLBSU and invited him to Monday night's meeting.

When we had made our arrangements, he gave my shoulder an affectionate squeeze, said "Nice to have really met you," and went back to his friends.

"He seems nice," Anna said.

"He does, doesn't he? It's funny; I had never really noticed him before."

"Well, if you don't mind my saying so —" Max began.

"And she's gonna say it whether you mind or not," Anna laughed.

Max shot her a mock evil look. "If you don't mind my saying so, there's been a lot you haven't noticed, what with your spending every waking moment brooding about Sarah. Dante didn't pine for Beatrice as badly as you obsess over that girl."

As much as I hated to admit it, she did have a point. I had spent all this time thinking that without Sarah I had nothing. Well, I did have my friends. And friends were definitely something.

Chapter 8

Journal Entry: Disaster Date #2

I was sitting in my apartment Sunday afternoon grading freshman papers that all seemed to begin with the phrase "In today's modern society . . ." when the phone rang. It was Max, exulting that she had found the perfect woman for me.

Apparently, after they had left Expressions, Max and Anna had stayed up the remaining half of the night trying to figure out a way to get my pathetic ass laid. And then it dawned on them: Circe and I would be perfect together.

"Circe? Give me a break! Is that her real name?"

"No, but her real name is so awful you can't blame her for changing it. You're gonna love her, Jess."

I cradled the phone on my shoulder and grabbed a Diet Coke from the fridge. "How do you know her?"

"She's an ex of mine."

"So now you're passing your rejects along to me?"

"I didn't dump her; she dumped me. She's great, really. She's a massage therapist — gives back rubs to die for. Anyway, she wants to meet you tonight at the Café Caffeine at 9:00."

"I don't know, Max. I've got papers to grade."

"So grade 'em now, and be at the Café Caffeine at 9:00."

"You and Anna will be there, too, right?"

"Think again, Jess. You know how ballistic Anna goes when she's around somebody I've slept with. It'll go much more smoothly if it's just the two of you."

"I don't know — "

"No whining, no excuses. Be there. Oh, and she'll be wearing black."

As I should've remembered, wearing black wasn't much of a distinguishing trait at the Café Caffeine. Everybody was wearing black: black leather jackets, black turtlenecks, black dresses, black jeans, for God's sake. It looked like a professional mourner's convention.

Not knowing what else to do, I sat down at an empty table and ordered a cappuccino. Just what I needed — something to make me jumpier. Within seconds, a woman strode confidently up to my table.

71

Her dyed black hair was short and spiky, and silver hoops sparkled in her nose, lower lip, and right eyebrow. Her black-lined eyes peered at me from behind a pair of rhinestone-studded cat's-eye glasses. She had the most heavily accessorized face I had ever seen.

She held out her hand. Silver rings decorated each finger, and her chewed fingernails were painted the color of fresh blood. "You must be Jess."

"Circe, I presume?" Was that what the unsuspecting Odysseus had said to her namesake? "Please, sit."

She sat. Her black minidress was cut low, and she certainly wasn't lacking in the cleavage department. A tiny double-woman's symbol was tattooed just above her left breast. I surveyed her black hair, her gothic makeup, and jewelry. She really was kind of sexy, in a Morticia Addams sort of way.

"So . . ." we said at the same time, then laughed.

"First dates really suck, huh?" she said, grinning.

"Yeah, pretty much." I thought back to the date with Jennifer and was relieved there were no controversial food decisions to be made. Of course, I didn't think Circe would get too upset over meat-eating, since her fashion statement basically said "I drink the blood of the living."

She fished in her tiny black purse. "You mind if I smoke?"

I shook my head, and she lit up. "Yeah, first dates suck. I hate all that small talk, all that getting-to-know-you chitchat bullshit you have to do after you determine you're actually attracted to the person." She leaned toward me. "I am attracted to you, by the way."

My face was probably the color of her nail polish.

"Uh, well, thank you. I, uh . . . you're not so bad your-self." In my mind, I was kicking myself.

She smiled. "You're nervous as a cat, aren't you? That's OK. It's cute. You know, there are ways we can get to know each other besides talking."

My stomach lurched in terror.

"Now, now, you naughty girl. That's not what I was talking about. I was going to suggest we dance."

"But there's no music —"

"Not here. At this place I know. Did you bring your car?"

"No, I walked."

"Good. I'll drive then." She was already up and out the door. I scurried behind her like a Chihuahua trying to keep up with a pit bull.

Her car was a sleek black MG convertible with the top down, despite the fact that it was far from warm outside.

"Hop in," she said, wrapping a black babushka around her head and lighting another cigarette. I slid into the passenger seat and fumbled with my seat belt, wishing I could radiate the same bohemian insouciance that practically oozed from this woman's pores.

As soon as she started the car, a blast of sound issued from the speakers that made me jump like I had been nearly missed in a drive-by shooting. Dissonant guitars shrieked, and female voices yowled like psychotic cats in heat, backed by percussion that sounded like it was being performed by toddlers with pots and pans.

"WHOM ARE WE LISTENING TO?" I yelled over the racket as we pulled out into traffic.

"BLOODY SHOW. DO YOU KNOW THEM?" she hollered.

"NO, I DON'T THINK SO."

Thankfully, she turned the volume down a notch. "They rock. Whom do you listen to?"

"Um, dyke patron saints, mostly — Janis Joplin, Patti Smith."

She curled her lip in a sneer, making me decide against telling her I was also a huge Loretta Lynn fan. "Boomer shit, huh? Well, I'll make you a tape. Maybe I can bring you into this century." Turning her attention to the car in front of her, she lay down on the horn. "Hey, buddy, could you maybe move before I reach menopause?"

Reckless isn't quite the word to describe Circe's driving. She wove her tiny car in and out of traffic, ran stop signs, and made turns that were not only illegal but improbable. I began to wonder if the reason she listened to such loud music in the car was to drown out the honks and curses of her fellow drivers. In order to stave off a panic attack, I tried to pretend I was on Mister Toad's Wild Ride at Walt Disney World.

Finally we arrived at our destination, a club called Sprockets in a decrepit area of downtown beside the railroad tracks. "This place is practically my second address," Circe said as we got out of the car in front of the club. As I walked around the back of her car, I noticed a bumper sticker that read I BRAKE FOR AMAZONS. It was good to know she would brake for something.

Sprockets was tiny, dark, and loud. Music that was primarily composed of bleeps and gurgles blared out of huge speakers, and writhing couples — female/female, male/male, and even the odd male/female — crowded a dance floor the size of my living room rug. They wore black velvet, black leather, black crepe, black, black, black. In my long, floral print dress and clogs, I felt like a time traveler from Woodstock.

"Come on, let's dance," Circe yelled over the bleeping music, grabbing my hand and pulling me toward the dance floor.

"Uh, it's kinda crowded up there, isn't it?"

"That's part of the fun — hot, sweaty bodies rubbing up against each other. Come on!"

Before I could protest, she had dragged me onto the floor. The music was gurgling like the sound a lava lamp might make, and I stood there, looking around at all the wiggling bodies, trying desperately to find the seemingly nonexistent beat.

I'm not much of a dancer. Don't get me wrong; when I'm alone in my apartment and I put the first side of Patti Smith's "Horses" on my scratchy old LP player, I can really rock out. But public dancing is another matter. Perhaps it's a throwback to my Baptist upbringing, but when confronted by a public dance floor, I freeze like a bird standing in oncoming traffic who suddenly forgets it knows how to fly.

Finally, I resorted to a stiff, little half-assed dance like high school boys do at the prom: I stepped to the left, then to the right semirhythmically, all the while looking as if I might snap my fingers but never actually doing so. Meanwhile Circe was all over the floor, wriggling and writhing, bumping and grinding, and generally letting her backbone slip, as they say in the old rhythm-and-blues songs. She looked sexy. Free.

Everybody was probably thinking what a stiff her date was. As if she were reading my mind, she leaned over and stage-whispered, "Loosen up, girl."

Trying to be obliging, I moved my hips a little. She disappeared, and I felt her behind me, her hands on my hips, her breasts pressing against my back. She moved me with her, her hips and my hips swaying smoothly, sinuously. When I closed my eyes, leaning my head back onto her shoulder, I forgot to be embarrassed. For a few minutes, I even forgot to think about Sarah. Instead, there was only Circe's body and mine moving in ways I didn't even know I could move and the music drowning all my inhibitions.

We must have danced for an hour. When we finally took a break and sat down with our beers, Circe said, "I knew you could dance."

I smiled, hoping I wasn't blushing.

"I bet you can do other things, too."

Good God, where did this girl get her confidence from, and what the hell was I supposed to say to that?

Fortunately, I didn't have to say anything, because at that moment a tall, extremely attractive black woman ran up to Circe, planted a big kiss on her cheek, and said something that I couldn't make out over the blasting music but sounded like something about "breaking a new one in."

When her friend returned to the dance floor, Circe said, "There's something I need to ask you, Jess." She peeled off a piece of the label on her beer bottle, then looked back up at me. "How do you feel about pain?"

Call me an idiot, but I had no idea what she was

talking about. "What — you mean like going-to-the-dentist pain or, like, spraining-your-ankle pain?"

She lit a cigarette and rolled her eyes in exasperation. "Jess, wake up. I'm talking about sex here."

"Omigod! Are you talking about whips and chains and stuff?"

She took on a testily patient tone, a wine connoisseur trying to explain her tastes to someone who only drinks wine from a box. "No, not chains, really. Leather restraints, a few whips — a riding crop, a cat-o'-nine, nothing too scary." She touched my hand. "Look, I can tell this is all new to you, but I'd love to initiate you. I'll be very gentle."

I couldn't help myself. "Gentle? With a whip?"

"Oh, God, you're not one of those women who's going to give me a lecture on how oppressive my sexuality is, are you?"

"Oh, no, it's not that. Whatever two consenting adults want to do is cool with me. It's just that . . . I've only had plain old regular sex with one woman once, and I'm not sure I'm ready to move on to something so . . . sophisticated." I chose that last word very carefully, wanting neither to sound judgmental nor to reveal my terror at the prospect of consenting to have the crap beaten out of me.

"OK, that's cool," she said. "I'm disappointed, but that's cool."

We danced a little more after that, but it wasn't the same. The aroma of seduction was no longer permeating the air. Finally, she offered to drive me home.

As we careened through traffic, I said, "You know, if you handle a whip the same way you handle a steering wheel, I bet you're some kinda badass."

She laughed, then after a while said, "Jess, I want to tell you something I've noticed about you." She lit a cigarette and inhaled thoughtfully. "You're really funny, and that's great, but sometimes you hide behind your humor to avoid your fears."

"Yeah? So?" I knew humor was one of my favorite defense mechanisms, but I didn't know I made it so obvious.

"Sometimes it's good to confront those fears."

"I'm not sure I understand what you're saying."

She brought the car to a screeching halt outside my apartment building. "What I'm saying is..." She touched my cheek gently. "Why don't you give me a call some time when you're not so fresh off the farm?"

In bed that night, I thought about Circe. I wondered if the energy we generated on the dance floor would be anything like the energy that we would generate in the bedroom. But then I saw myself, chained to the wall like a victim of the Spanish Inquisition, while a leather-clad Circe wielded a bullwhip menacingly. My imagination stopped right at the point when the leather bit into my skin.

OK, so maybe Circe had a point. I was scared. Scared and maybe a little repressed. But was a distaste for being beaten black-and-blue necessarily something I needed to overcome in order to be a healthy, well-adjusted adult?

This dating thing was so damned complicated. First, I go out with someone who acts like I'm clubbing baby seals just because I'm eating crabmeat, and then there's the Marquis de Sade who acts like

I'm some kind of repressed, old-maid schoolteacher because I won't let her club me!

As I tried to fall asleep, I pictured Jennifer's scrubbed, Ivory-girl face, then Circe's pierced, sneering, blood-red lips. But the face that finally sent me off to dreamland belonged to Sarah.

Chapter 9

When I met Christopher at the GLBSU meeting, I was surprised to see that Amanda and B. J. weren't there. They never missed a meeting. It was like going to church and finding the two most pious Sunday school teachers absent. When I got home, I called their number, but nobody was home, and their answering machine was either turned off or not working.

The topic of Monday night's meeting had been fund-raising, and as a result, Chris and I now found ourselves manning and womanning the table at the GLBSU's first bake sale. It's a fact of life: If you join an organization, whether it's left wing or right wing or in between, sooner or later you're going to find yourself participating in a bake sale.

It was lunch rush at the student center, and it was fascinating to observe people's reactions to our table. They were inevitably drawn by the sight of the cookies and brownies and Rice Krispies treats, but when they saw the sign that read GAY, LESBIAN, AND BISEXUAL STUDENT UNION, one of three things happened: They smiled supportively and bought the goodies, they shrugged dismissively and bought the goodies, or they recoiled in horror and skittered away.

Christopher was telling me about his dissertation proposal. "So I'm hoping the powers that be will let me write it on gay and lesbian literature." He stopped talking when he saw a baseball cap-wearing fraternity boy shifting his gaze back and forth between the brownies and the sign announcing the nature of our organization. "Would you like to try a Grand Marnier brownie?" Christopher asked. "They're baked by real fags."

The frat boy reddened a little and grinned. "Yeah, OK, I'll take one."

Christopher leered as the boy walked away, munching. "I knew he could be had."

I laughed. "You're a smooth talker, you know that?"

"Believe me, honey, my talk doesn't sell anything but brownies."

"I find that hard to believe."

"Oh, it's been a long, dry season ever since I

moved to this town." He helped himself to a chocolate chip cookie and dropped a quarter into the money box. "I did my master's at UK, and I had a boyfriend there who was also in the English department. He was smart, gorgeous, built like a brick —" He looked up at a young woman who was clearly lingering over the baked goods as an excuse to eavesdrop. He smiled at her supersweetly. "It's the damnedest thing," he said. "Keebler Company has elves that make their cookies, but real, live fairies make ours!"

"Hey," I interrupted, "those cookies weren't made by fairies. They were made by me and Betty Crocker."

Christopher shot me a sly glance. "I had no idea you and Betty were so close."

The young woman skittered away.

"OK," I said, "now that you've succeeded in scaring off a paying customer, tell me more about your boyfriend."

"Ex-boyfriend," he emphasized. "Well, as is often the case with pretty people, he wanted to share his prettiness with the world, not just with me."

"You mean he —"

"Couldn't keep it in his pants? Yes, that's exactly what I mean." He grinned. "I see delicacy will get me nowhere. So anyway, I have the unfortunate affliction of being a one-man man, and after a while, I just couldn't take it anymore. I applied to the Ph.D. program here because I couldn't stand to be in the same town with the boy."

"That's too bad."

"Ah, well, I try not to dwell on it. I refuse to subscribe to the 'tragic diva' school of homosexuality."

He pinched up a few brownie crumbs and popped them into his mouth.

Out of the corner of my eye I saw Grady Combs coming out of the bookstore. "Omigod, Christopher, cover me!" I ducked behind him so Grady couldn't see my face.

"Is there a lone gunman somewhere I'm not seeing?"

"There might as well be. See that guy over there who looks kind of like David Crosby? He's talking to the shaved-headed guy in the suit?"

"Yeah?"

"That's Grady Combs from my comp class. Don't let his stuck-in-the-seventies appearance fool you; his personal philosophy is pure Ronald Reagan."

"People should really be required to match their fashion statements to their politics. It's so much less confusing that way." My head was still ducked. "It's OK. He gave the guy he was talking to a book and left."

"It was probably *Mein Kampf.* It's so annoying to have somebody that annoying in class. Do you know what he said the other day? He actually said that he admitted that there were some good black people."

"How progressive of him." He rolled his eyes. "Life's too short to waste time talking about idiots. So what I want to know is, is there anybody special in your life?"

"Well, there's somebody who's special to me, but . . ." I trailed off. "It's all very 'tragic diva,' I'm afraid."

"That's OK. The tragic diva thing is always more

novel on a lesbian. On a gay man, it's just a cliché. So go ahead, sister, sing your song of woe."

"Um, well, OK." I took a breath. "Her name is Sarah."

"How literary, like *Patience and Sarah.*"

"Actually, it's more like *impatience* with Sarah.' We were best friends in college, we slept together once, and then boom! She's suddenly engaged."

"Not to you or a person of your gender, I take it."

"You take it correctly."

He patted my knee. "Well, look on the bright side, honey. If sex with you scared her so badly she had to retreat to the enemy camps, she must've liked it."

"I had no idea you were such a Pollyanna."

"Well, now you know. Would you like to play the Glad Game?"

As it turned out, I played the Sad Game instead. Relieved to find an impartial ear, I whined about Sarah, about my two disastrous dates, about how I just didn't understand city women. I spilled my guts for twenty minutes straight, pausing only to sell the occasional Rice Krispies treat.

After I had finished, Christopher said, "May I ask you a question, Jess?"

"Sure."

"When you're at home alone, what do you fix yourself for dinner?"

"What does that have to do with —"

"Humor me."

"Oh, I don't know. A can of soup or Ramen noodles. Maybe a tunafish sandwich." ·

"That's what I thought. You never cook a nice dinner when you eat alone, do you?"

"Well, no. I mean, what would be the point?"

"The point is, you might enjoy it. All your happiness doesn't have to come from other people. Sarah may come around or she may not. In the meantime, try not to wallow in your own misery. Do something you know will bring you pleasure. Take a walk through Old Louisville. Buy yourself a new CD. Get a pet. Make a big pot of spaghetti carbonara for dinner —"

"I don't even know what's in spaghetti carbonara."

He rolled his eyes. "That's not the point. The point is, you've got to learn how to enjoy your own company."

"Is Christopher doing his impression of *Life's Little Instruction Book* again?" We looked up. It was Alex, the GLBSU president.

Christopher smiled at him. "Can I help it if I'm omnipotent?"

I laughed. "Well, after that therapy session, I feel like I ought to at least buy you a cookie."

He clutched his stomach. "Trust me. If I eat another one, the phrase *tossing one's cookies* will take on an all-too-literal meaning. You want to walk back to humanities with me? Only thirty minutes 'til our thrilling history of criticism class."

"I'll catch up with you in class. I've got to pick up something at the bookstore."

At the bookstore, I bought a picture postcard of Dorothy Parker. I sat down on a cold bench outside the student center and scrawled out a note.

Sarah,

Mrs. Parker and I say hi. I've been too busy to write you a full-fledged letter, but I think of you always. Best wishes to you and Mike.

Love,
Jess

I read back over it. It was very restrained, I thought. I wished her well on her engagement, and I didn't even make mention of the Dorothy Parker poem that had caused me to select that particular postcard:

Oh, life is a glorious cycle of song,
A vast extemporanea,
And love is a thing that can never go wrong,
And I am Marie of Roumania.

Although, I must admit, my first instinct had been to sign the card *Marie of Roumania.* But restraint was important. If I didn't hold my love and anger in check, I'd lose Sarah altogether, and I couldn't handle that. I stuck a stamp on the postcard and dropped it in the mailbox. Now maybe I was ready to start following some of Christopher's advice.

I took a shortcut through a backstreet on my way home from school. Walking by the Dumpsters was always fascinating. On any given day, perfectly good furniture and easily fixable appliances would be shoved up against a Dumpster, ready to be hauled away. I imagined that the Dumpsters themselves probably contained clothes that were still wearable and food that was still edible. I never investigated, of course, because the streets were filled with people who needed the stuff far worse than I did.

Today, for example, a big, lime-green armchair was sitting in the alley. The chair was ugly, certainly not *Architectural Digest* material, but it looked comfortable, the kind of chair that actually does give you the room to curl up with a good book. As I walked closer to the chair, I saw something in it — a little ball of fur almost the same color as a pink grapefruit. The ball shifted, and a pair of light blue eyes looked up at me. The kitten was curled up in that chair just as casually as if it were in someone's living room.

I squatted down for a better look. Her little eyes were bright, but she was skinny enough to shimmy through a drinking straw. "Hey, sweetie," I crooned. I stretched my fingers out under her nose so she could smell me. "You're not rabid or anything, are you?"

"Mew?" she replied. She sniffed daintily at my fingers. I scratched behind her ears, and her purr revved up into full gear. For such a tiny kitty, she purred like the motor of a Harley-Davidson. The poor little thing, I thought — abandoned by someone she had trusted. I could relate.

I thought about Christopher's advice: Get a pet. Finding this little fuzzball was definitely a sign. Synchronicity or serendipity or whatever it's called. Without another thought, I scooped the little critter up and tucked her inside my jacket.

At my apartment, I poured her a saucer of milk. She lapped it up as greedily as her cat dignity would allow. While she drank, I reached for the phone. "Hey, Christopher? You know how you told me I should get a pet?"

"Among other things, yes."

"Well, on my way home, I found myself a genuine, full-blooded Dumpster kitty." I glanced over at her. Finished with her milk, she was now striking an elaborate pose which allowed her to wash between the toes of her left back foot. "God, she's so cute."

"Jess, this is a good move," Christopher said. "But there's just one thing."

"What's that?"

"If you name her Sarah, I'll kill you."

Chapter 10

Pink-grapefruit kitty (as I had been calling her) stood rigidly on the metal examination table in the vet's office. Anna, wearing the scrub suit that was her veterinary assistant's uniform, stroked the kitty under her chin and puckered her lips to croon, "You're a booful kitty-kitty, yes, you are."

"I still don't know what I'm going to name her," I said.

Anna peeked beneath the kitty's tail. "Well, here's a helpful hint. It's not a her."

"Omigod, really? It never even occurred to me it

could be a boy. I guess on some subconscious level, I think of all dogs as boys and all cats as girls."

Anna laughed. "Well, I'm all for the lesbian nation, even among the feline population." She looked down at pink-grapefruit kitty and cooed, "But if all kitties were girls, we wouldn't have all those cute little baby kitties, isn't that wight, Mr. Tom Kitten?"

"I can't believe he's a boy. He just seemed so . . . feminine. I feel just like the Stephen Rea character in *The Crying Game*."

Anna seemed lost in thought for a moment, then said, "You know, I've often thought the world would be a better place if we neutered some men the way we neuter boy kitties. Not all men, of course, just the ones with ETS."

"ETS?"

"Excessive testosterone syndrome."

"Oh, so like, guys who shoot helpless deer just so they can mount their heads on the wall and use their hooves as gun racks —"

"Neuter 'em. And of course, we'd neuter wife beaters, rapists . . ."

"Gay bashers, KKK members, Grady Combs in my comp class . . ." I chimed in.

"They'd be so docile then," Anna said dreamily, "just like big, fat, lazy neutered tom kitties."

Dr. Adams, a gentle man whom Anna and I would definitely not neuter, walked in then. "Well, it looks like good news," he said, glancing down at his clipboard. "No signs of feline leukemia or any other diseases. So we'll just get your kitty vaccinated here, and then you can take him home and give him a name."

Anna held the kitty while Dr. Adams slipped a hypodermic needle into the loose flesh over the kitty's shoulder. He didn't even flinch.

"Well, Jess," Dr. Adams said. "I think we're all set." He gave the kitty a quick pat. "So many stray cats die on the streets every year. It's always nice to see one get a good home."

"When do I need to bring him back?"

"He won't need any more shots for a full year, but I imagine you'll want to make an appointment in a couple of months or so. That is, of course, if you want to have him neutered."

Anna and I erupted in a fit of giggles worthy of two junior-high schoolgirls.

That night, I sat at the computer typing up a short paper for my introduction to scholarship class. Pink-grapefruit kitty was curled around the back of my neck like a fur collar, purring to beat the band. I glanced over at my bookshelf in hopes of finding a quotation to juice up my rather dry essay, and then I saw a book by the author who would become my dainty male kitty's namesake.

"You," I said, reaching up to rub his velvety nose, "are Oscar Wildcat."

He mewed appreciatively.

Just as I was printing up my paper, there was a knock at the door. It was a little past 11:00 — kind of late for unannounced visitors on a weeknight. I opened the door to find B. J. looking rumpled and weary. Her face was blotchy, and her eyes were puffy and shadowed from exhaustion.

"B. J., I've been trying to call you all week, but nobody was home and your machine wouldn't kick on."

"Um, well, that's because nobody lives there anymore."

"What?"

She leaned against the door facing. "Uh, can I come in?"

"Oh, sure. Sorry. You want a beer or something?"

"Yeah, a beer'd be good."

When I handed her the beer, she looked up at me with wet, red eyes and whispered, "We broke up, Jess."

"What? Who broke up?" It was an idiotic response, but B. J.'s obvious distress had me all discombobulated.

"Amanda and me. Who the hell do you think?" She buried her face in her hands, and big sobs shook her muscular little body.

There are few sights more pitiful than a crying butch. If you see a butch crying, you know she'd hold it in if she could, but she's finally reached the point where she just can't hold back any longer. Not knowing what else to do, I sat down beside her and put my arm around her. She clung to me immediately, burying her face in my chest like an insecure child, soaking my T-shirt with tears.

She cried in silence for a long time, then finally looked up and said, "She left me for Sal."

I racked my brain for a few seconds. "Sal from the bar?"

"Uh-huh." She sat up and used her shirttail to wipe her eyes.

"Jesus, what is she thinking? Sal's got problems."

"Yeah, but see, that's what Amanda likes." She fished around in her jacket pocket. "You care if I smoke?"

I shook my head and went to fetch her a saucer to use as an ashtray. When I came back, little Oscar was curled up on her lap.

"Maybe I should just get a cat," B. J. said. "They're easier to look after than a woman."

"Yep, just feed 'em and change their litter, and they're fine."

When B. J. exhaled her first stream of smoke, Oscar squinted up at her and then minced away, offended. "Amanda didn't like me smoking neither," B. J. said, more to Oscar than to me. "I quit for her." She took another drag. "The thing is, Jess, what you said about Sal having problems . . . It's like problems are what turns Amanda on. You got problems, she wants to fix 'em. If you don't have problems, she'll invent some for you and then fix those."

"What do you mean?"

"Well, it's like . . . when she met me I was an orderly over at St. Joe's. I liked being an orderly, helping out, being part of the team, you know. But once me and Amanda started dating, it was like me being an orderly wasn't good enough. I wasn't — how did she say it? — 'living up to my potential.' She also wanted me to quit smoking and quit eating greasy food. So I turn around and all of a sudden, I don't smoke, I eat rabbit food instead of cheeseburgers, and I'm at State studying to be a nurse."

"So going back to college was all Amanda's idea?"

"Yeah, only there wasn't no 'back' to it. I had never gone to college, never wanted to go to college. I was just glad I made it through high school. I know you must like school because you've been in it for-fuckin'-ever, Jess. But I hate it. Always did."

"Yeah, well, it's not for everybody."

93

"It's not for me, that's for damn sure. When Amanda thought I was being a good little student, everything was great between us . . . lots of hugging and kissing, sex like you wouldn't believe. But the thing was, I never was a good little student. I cut classes and hung out in the student center. I didn't turn in assignments. And when I got my mid-term report with all unsatisfactory marks on it, Amanda lost her shit."

She shook her head in exasperation and lit another cigarette. "That's when things started to go real sour. I tried to tell her I didn't want to be a student in the first place, that I had never wanted to be a nurse. But she was just so mad I wasn't, she said, 'growing.' "

"Yeah, but she meant changing." I scooped up Oscar and cuddled him. "I never knew Amanda had such a Pygmalion complex."

"Huh?"

"I mean, she's like Henry Higgins in *My Fair Lady*."

"You're probably right. I don't know. I don't see movies much. But not long after she found out I was doing bad in school, she started staying out a lot at night. At the library, studying, she said. Studying — unlike some people. Well, it turns out, what she was studying was Sal."

I touched her hand. "I'm so sorry, B. J."

She laughed bitterly. "You know, she's already got Sal in one of them twelve-step programs. Next thing you know, she'll have her in school studying to be a substance abuse counselor or some kinda shit like that."

I smiled. "You're probably right."

"You know," she said, "I've had thirteen girlfriends since I first came out back in high school, and I don't think a single one of them loved me for who I really am." Tears welled in her eyes. "Someday, though . . ."

"Yeah," I said, wishing for myself, too, "someday."

"But anyway," she said, grabbing her jacket, "the real reason I came by was to tell you I'm moving. One of the hospitals over in Cincinnati is expanding, and they're hiring all kinds of staff, so I thought I'd try my luck over there. I've already dated and broken up with every damn woman in this town." She looked into my eyes for a second, and it felt so intimate I had to look away. "Every damn woman but you, that is. And if you've got a thing for the straight girls, you sure as hell wouldn't like me." She shrugged into her jacket.

"I do like you, B. J."

"Yeah," she said. "Just not that way." She gave me a chaste peck on the cheek. "Thanks for letting me boo-hoo. And look me up in Cincinnati."

"I'll do that."

I watched her walk down the hall. When she let the outside door slam behind her, I moved to my window and watched her shuffle dejectedly down the street, her shoulders hunched in her black leather jacket, until she was out of view.

Chapter 11

Journal Entry

Amanda and B. J.'s breakup has gotten to me more than I expected. It probably sounds silly, but I thought they'd be together forever. The air between them positively zinged with sexual electricity, and they were always touching, even if it was just their knees or arms brushing each other. When I was with them, there was always something tugging at me, telling me I should probably leave so they could be alone.

I guess what I'm saying is, if Amanda and B. J.
break up, what hope is there for the rest of us? Maybe
it's just human nature to fuck up relationships, to
leave when you think you've found a perfect love with
someone whose annoying habits you don't know yet. I
still think about Sarah every damned second even
though her annoying habit is that she thinks she's
straight. Well, at least I'm committed. Or maybe I
should be committed. Or maybe . . .

The phone rang.

"So are you coming to this party tonight or
what?" Christopher asked.

"I don't know." I cradled the receiver on my
shoulder. "English department parties really aren't my
scene."

"Well, they're not my scene either, hon, but if I
don't go, I'm gonna flunk Departmental Politics 101,
and you know what that means."

"I'm afraid I don't."

"Of course, you don't. You're just an M.A. student,
which means the powers that be will probably let you
slide on through the system whether you suck up or
not. I'm a Ph.D. student. If I don't kiss butt at every
available opportunity, they won't let me graduate."

"And so why should I, a lowly M.A. student, go?"

"To make the experience bearable. Afterward we
can go somewhere for coffee and dish dirt about
everybody at the party."

The party was held in the sprawling Victorian
house of Rick Sanders, Louisville State's foremost
creative writing professor and poet-in-residence. I had
never spoken with Professor Sanders, although I had

seen him striding across campus, wearing dark sunglasses and sucking on a cigarette as though its essence was poetic inspiration itself. With his chiseled features and smooth manner, his image was more like that of Steve Dallas in the *Bloom County* cartoons than, say, e. e. cummings. With his wife, poet Jill Madison, Professor Sanders had founded a new literary journal, *Barbaric Yawp!*, the masthead of which read, "poetry on the edge . . . on the edge of a new millennium."

Professor Sanders answered the door. He was missing his sunglasses, revealing a pair of small, rather piggy eyes, but he did have his cigarette. "Hi, Christopher!" He gave Christopher a companionable, straight-guy slap on the back, and I watched as Christopher tried not to flinch. "Glad you could make it!" He turned his attentions to me. "I've seen you around the department, but I don't believe we've had the pleasure of meeting."

"Jess Hamlin."

"Well, glad you could make it, Jess," he said, completing his welcoming shtick. "Come in, come in. There's beer in the fridge and food on the table."

The living room was filled with graduate students talking about the same things they talked about in the office (critical theory, pedagogy, et al.), the only differences being that they were drinking beer instead of coffee and sitting on comfortable furniture.

A pudgy, bearded GTA who seemed to be having a heated discussion with a woman who looked like she could star in *Pippi Longstocking Goes to Grad School* said, "Hey, Christopher. We were just having an argument about Q Theory. Maybe you can settle it for us."

"Fag Man to the rescue," Christopher said, leaping right into their conversation and leaving me standing there like the proverbial bastard at the family reunion.

Since I was clueless as to what they were talking about (something about "the gaze" or "the gays"), I decided to search for the aforementioned beer. I was prepared to fall back into a habit I'd established in my college years — using alcohol as a social lubricant.

In the kitchen, a petite woman with long, ash-blond hair was arranging pita bread on a platter. She spun around to face me, looking startled. "Oh . . . hi."

"Hi. I'm sorry — I didn't mean to scare you."

"It's not your fault. Parties make me nervous. To use appropriate clichés, I'm kind of a lone wolf; Rick's the social butterfly." From the looks of the glass of amber liquid in her hand, she was using alcohol as a social lubricant, too. "I'm Jill, by the way." She smiled, displaying a row of tiny, evenly spaced teeth.

Jill looked to be several years older than her husband. Her face had a few fine lines, and the skin on her neck had loosened with age. She wore a short, roomy, flowered dress, and her legs were covered with surprisingly thick, downy hair. A silver-belled ankle bracelet jingled as she shifted one of her bare feet. This woman, I thought, bakes her own bread.

"I'm Jess. I'm an M.A. student in the department."

She nodded pleasantly, seeming unsure of what to say, opened a cabinet over the sink, and retrieved a bottle of Usher's White Label scotch. She refilled her glass. "Can I offer you a drink?"

"I'm not much of a scotch drinker, but I will take

a beer." Scotch, a drink I associated with cigar-smoking businessmen, didn't seem to fit Jill somehow; she'd look much more at home with a cup of herb tea.

As I opened the refrigerator door, I sensed a feline presence at my feet. I looked down to see a beautiful, long-haired, black cat with eyes the color of copper pennies. "Aren't you gorgeous?" I said, squatting down to pet her.

"That's Midnight," Jill said. "Our son Caleb named her. It's kind of pathetic, two poets who are always searching for fresh ways of saying things, living under the same roof with a black cat named Midnight."

I laughed.

"Well, after hearing *Goodnight Moon* for the third time, the little man finally started to nod off."

The voice sounded vaguely familiar. I looked up and realized the voice belonged to Michelle, the woman whose impressively bulging bicep I had felt at the Starlite. God, that seemed like ages ago.

"Oh, hey. Jess, right?" She sounded as surprised to see me as I was to see her.

"Yeah. Hey, Michelle. You're about the last person I expected to see here."

"You two know each other?" Jill's tone was bright, but there was an uneasiness behind it.

"Yeah, we've met."

A droopy-eyed little boy in Batman pajamas padded into the kitchen. "Mom, I'm starving."

Jill took a fortifying sip of her drink. "You can grab some carrot sticks off the buffet, but then you have to go to sleep."

He ran into the dining room and grabbed a double handful of carrot sticks. "Will you tuck me in, Mom?"

"But you said you wanted Auntie Michelle to tuck you in."

"But now I want you to do it," he said, between crunches of carrot.

Jill set down her drink. "This time you have to promise you'll stay in bed."

"I promise," he said, holding up three fingers. "Scout's honor."

"OK then, scout," Jill said. "Up the stairs with you."

I wondered if she really cast a worried glance in Michelle's and my direction or if it was just my imagination.

Alone in the kitchen, Michelle and I smiled awkwardly at each other. "So . . ." I began, but then realized I had no idea what to say.

"So, it's good to see you," she filled in the blank.

"Yeah, you too. You look great." I felt stupid for blurting that out, but it was the truth. Her braids were woven with shells and beads, and she wore an emerald-green silk pantsuit. "Um, I'm sorry I never called you. I've been really busy with school, and —"

"Don't worry about it." She opened the fridge and helped herself to a beer. "Say, you want to take a little walk with me out back? I'm feeling kinda claustrophobic in here."

"Sure," I said, hearing the drone of the theorizing and pontificating coming from the living room. "I could use some fresh air."

The back porch was empty, so we settled on the swing. "So," Michelle began, "I take it these little smarty parties aren't exactly your idea of a good time."

We began swaying back and forth gently. "Is it that obvious?" I had been trying to hide my discomfort.

"Oh, I'm probably just projecting. Of course, I was hiding upstairs with the five-year-old child, and you were in the kitchen with the cat, so I think that says something about our status as party people."

I laughed. "Well, at least at this kind of party."

"Exactly. I stayed in the living room until I got tired of all the white boys expecting me to be the Voice of the Black People. They tried to be subtle about it, saying, you know, 'So, Michelle, what do you think of Zora Neale Hurston's idealization of white beauty?' Of course, they weren't really asking, 'what do you think?' as much as 'what do your people think?' I got tired of acting as the spokesperson for millions and hid upstairs with the kid. The hardest question he's gonna ask me is, Where do babies come from? That one, I can handle."

I laughed. "I just came because my friend Christopher dragged me here —"

"Gagged, bound, and struggling?"

"Pretty much." I sipped my beer. "So how did you end up here? I mean, there's nobody's butt you need to kiss, right?"

She grinned, rather sheepishly, I thought. "Lord, how did I end up here? You ask some hard questions, lady." She downed her beer, then said, "It's a long story, so stop me when you get bored. I met Jill because I answered an ad she put in the *Arts Musepaper*."

"An ad? You mean, like, 'married white female seeks —' "

"A babysitter for five-year-old son."

"Oh, that kind of ad."

She playfully slapped my thigh. "Yes, that kind of ad, you nasty thing! My car needed a brake job, and I figured I could always fall back on my old high-school babysitting skills for extra money. So I started staying with Caleb a couple of times a week, and we got really close. He's a sweet kid." She looked down at her feet. "So are you bored yet?"

"Nope."

"Well, I also started talking to Jill. She'd invite me to stay for a drink after Caleb went to bed. Sometimes Rick would join us, but most of the time he wouldn't." She looked around, then lowered her voice. "I got the feeling she needed a friend — somebody who was outside of her and Rick's little artsy-fartsy social scene. I also got the feeling she was doing the white liberal thing, you know, thinking of me as her Black Friend and sort of congratulating herself for having one — telling Caleb to call me Auntie Michelle, inviting me to parties so her white liberal friends could see me. It's crazy, you know, you can't even have a friendship without the race thing coming up." She sighed. "But all that aside, I like Jill. She's a really good poet, and eventually I got up my nerve and showed her some of my work."

"I didn't know you were a poet."

"Hey, theater, poetry... If it doesn't pay jack-shit, I'm good at it. So anyway, after giving me a few revision suggestions, she and Rick end up publishing this poem I wrote in memory of Audre Lorde in the first issue of *Barbaric Yawp!*"

"I'd love to see some of your work," I said, actually meaning it. Most of the time, if someone tells me she's a poet, I can't run away fast enough. "Jill's sort of your mentor, then."

"Yeah, well, there's kind of more to it than that. Sometimes I wish there wasn't, though."

"What do you mean?"

She looked around to make sure no one was in earshot, and then spoke barely above a whisper. "Well, one night Rick was away at a weekend conference, and Jill was drunk, and I was lonely and a little drunk myself, and, well, things started happening."

"Things?"

She laughed. "Don't act all innocent with me, girl. You know damn well what kind of things."

"Does Rick know?"

"Doesn't know or doesn't care from all I can tell. When Rick's not off playing the Poet of the People, his little habit keeps him so busy he doesn't have much time for his wife or kid."

I thought of Rick's dark glasses, of the cigarette he held in a trembling hand. "You mean, like a drug habit?"

She smiled. "I like you, Jess. You really do have a naive side, don't you? Yep. He's got a drug habit, all right. Apparently, they're pretty deep in debt what with the expense of starting the magazine and all their income going up Rick's nose. He tells Jill he's not addicted, that the coke inspires him. It inspires him to be an asshole, in my opinion.

"So Jill turns to me for solace, and because I've not had a steady girlfriend since God was a boy, I turn that solace into sex. She alternates between clinging to me and crying that she's not a dyke." She shook her head and laughed. "So here I am. As if my own family wasn't bad enough, now I've gone and squeezed myself into a nice, middle-class, dysfunctional white family. So that's my little personal soap opera. You got one to share?"

"Not one to top yours."

The back door swung open. We both jumped as though we had been caught in some forbidden act. Jill stood with her drink in her hand, backlit by the kitchen's fluorescent lighting. "Oh, there you are, Michelle. I was afraid you had left." She cast a not-so-friendly glance in my direction. "I hope I'm not interrupting."

I rose from the swing. For a woman who claimed not to be a dyke, Jill was awfully possessive. "Not at all. We were just shooting the breeze."

In a real-life case of deus ex machina, Christopher appeared in the doorway. "Oh, so the little social butterfly is hiding on the back porch?"

"I'm more of a social caterpillar, actually."

"Well, are you ready to crawl back to your cocoon?"

I was more than ready to get away from Jill's suspicious glare. "Yeah, I guess so. Thanks for the hospitality, Jill. Nice to see you again, Michelle."

"Yeah, you too, Jess," Michelle said, looking as if she longed to escape with Christopher and me. "Oh, and say hey to your girlfriend for me — Sarah, right?"

"Yeah, right."

Christopher was barely out of Michelle's earshot when he said, "Girlfriend? You told her Sarah's your girlfriend?"

"Shh!" I hissed. "I'll explain it later."

"You really like to burn your bridges, don't you, Jess? I mean, why lie to her? She's really cute."

"Yeah," I said. "Don't remind me."

Chapter 12

Jess,
    Hi right back at you. This postcard's from the World of Coca-Cola. Mike and I went there this weekend. You should taste some of the drinks from other parts of the world they have there. Lichee nut soda — blecch! Everything's good here. I love the big city. (Who'd have guessed it, right?) Trouble is, I'm too busy to enjoy what it has to offer most of the time. Hope all's well with you.

Luv,
Sarah

The first thing I noticed about Sarah's postcard was that she used l-o-v-e in reference to Atlanta and l-u-v in reference to me. It was unlike her to "cutely" misspell a word. Even though Sarah's fashion sense always leaned toward the cute, her mind didn't. She had written l-u-v instead of l-o-v-e because she didn't want me to get the wrong idea, didn't want me to think she was relating to me as anything other than an old college pal.

As I often do when I'm depressed, I went to the stereo and put on a Janis Joplin LP. I always listen to Janis on vinyl; the scratchiness of the record complements the raw emotional content of her singing. Hers is a voice not to be digitally remastered.

I lay back on the futon and listened to "Pearl" howl out her blues, daring her lover to take another piece of her heart. Something about that song turned the idea of female masochism on its ear. There was power in Janis's pain, malice in her masochism.

As I listened, I grabbed a pen and paper and started writing. No thought seemed to move my pen; it moved on its own, scrawling violently across the page.

Dear Sarah,

How happy you must be. I picture you coming home from med school and having dinner with Mike and the two of you walking the streets of Buckhead hand in hand without a care in the world because, after all, what do two happy, soon-to-be married heterosexuals have to worry about? I know that's not fair; people in any type of relationship have plenty to worry about, but good God, at least the two of you can hold hands in public without having obscenities yelled at you.

*I miss you. I mean, when you've lived with some-
one for four years, eaten three meals a day together,
and fallen asleep in the same room every night — a
chitchatty little postcard just can't replace that, you
know? Sure, sometimes I wake up from a dream in
which I've been holding your perfect body like I did
that one perfect night, but mostly what I miss is the
day-to-day stuff, the security of a seemingly inseparable
friendship. I bet you miss it, too.*

*I mean, I know you have a day-to-day life with
Mike, but I wonder if you can have the kind of
intimacy with a man that we had together, or do you
always hold back a little, afraid of disclosing too
much, afraid of making the wrong impression, afraid
of losing him? Or am I totally off the mark here? Am
I just making these assumptions because I'm gay, and
you . . . I guess . . . are not?*

*The thing is, Sarah, there are no guarantees in
human relationships. Our inseparable friendship has
disintegrated into an exchange of friendly, dishonest
notes. My friends Amanda and B. J., who were so in
love they made everyone around them feel like voyeurs,
broke up. My friend Christopher's boyfriend left him.
Gay or straight, there's never an always and forever
you can just take for granted. Even when you put on
your white dress and your daddy escorts you down the
aisle and gives you away to the next man who'll own
you, and you say " 'til death do us part," you can
never be sure.*

*Have I always been this cynical? Didn't somebody
once say that a cynic was just a disappointed
romantic? You know, Sarah, I think I've even met
somebody I could like — I mean, like that way. Her
honesty is refreshing, like a tall glass of iced tea after*

I've been parched by secrets and lies and hypocrisy. And so what do I do? I get scared, and I lie to her. I tell her I'm seeing someone — you, specifically. It was on the day I found out about your and Mike's engagement, and I was so hurt, I felt like I was lying to protect myself. But to protect myself from what? A chance, however iffy, at happiness?

You know why human relationships are so tricky, Sarah? It's because one person by herself can fuck up her life pretty badly. Add another person into the equation, and you've got a disaster of biblical proportions.

If I were a witch, I'd cook up an anti-love potion, one that would make me stop dreaming of you, that would snuff out this little spark of hope that keeps burning for you and would leave me comfortably numb, like a shot of novocaine straight into my heart. I know this letter is shot through with venom, but most of my poison is pointed inward. Like Janis Joplin, I may rage and scream and growl and hiss, but those sounds are just another way of expressing a woman's heartbreak.

Jess

I dropped the letter in the kitchen sink, lit a match, and dropped it on top of it. I watched the paper curl and blacken. The taste of ashes filled my mouth.

Chapter 13

"You wanna get a pitcher?" Max hollered over the Pure Prairie League song that was blasting from the jukebox. We were at Ted's Tavern, the straight bar across the street from my apartment building. The barroom was dark and shoebox-shaped, with the required entertainments of a pool table and pinball machine. The only attempts at decoration were the neon beer signs that glowed against the dark, cheaply paneled walls.

"Yeah, why not?" I fished a couple of singles out

of my jacket pocket. "I'll babysit the pinball machine while you're gone."

Max grinned. "And then I'll come back and whip your ass."

The beer was of the tasteless megabrewery variety, but its coldness made it palatable, and Max delivered the promised ass-whipping several times. I still wasn't used to these newfangled pinball machines with their six flippers and lights and bleeps and blips — so different from the two-flipper, low-tech machines of my childhood.

"You wanna sit down for a while?" I asked after I'd lost my fourth game.

Max sniffed the air theatrically. "Is that surrender I smell?"

"What's that, the new fragrance from Calvin Klein?" We carried our pitcher and mugs to a booth in the corner. "How long is Anna gonna be gone?"

"It depends on how her grandma's surgery goes. To be honest, the prognosis doesn't sound good. Anna took the whole week off from work and told her professor what the deal was. I could be a bachelor woman for the rest of the week." She sipped her beer. "Domesticity spoils you, Jess. You get so used to not being alone, it's like if you spend an hour by yourself, your head will explode or something. It's pathetic."

"Yeah, so why do I envy you?"

"Don't blame me, woman. I've tried to do my part to put an end to your solitary state . . . which reminds me, you never did tell me about your date with Circe. Every time I've mentioned it, you've started wiggling like a bug under a pin."

"So now that you've got me all liquored up you're gonna get the truth out of me?"

"That's what I'm shooting for."

I swallowed some beer for courage. "Um, when you were dating Circe, was she into, like, whips and bondage and stuff?"

Max raised an eyebrow. "Well, nothing serious. I mean, she tied me up once or twice, but she never struck me as the dominatrix type. Or should I just say that she never struck me?"

"Well, your little girlfriend has grown up now. Her main getting-to-know-you question was, How do you feel about pain?"

Max slapped the table and hooted. "That one never came up on *The Dating Game*! Got any welts to show me?"

I stared down at the table, my face heating up.

"I take it that's not your scene. That's cool; it's not mine either, really. Of course, I'll try anything once. Hell, I even tried a man once. But if what you wanted to know was if I set you up with Circe knowing her Torquemada-like tendencies, no, I didn't. When we were dating, she wore black and read a lot of Anne Rice, but that was as kinky as she got." Max reached across the table and patted my hand. "So, to answer your question, no, I did not set you up with Circe because I have a subconscious desire to beat the crap out of you."

I laughed. "That's good to hear."

"Is this girl talk, or can I join in?" A scrawny, rather mangy man had appeared at our table.

Max regarded him coldly. "It's dyke talk."

He squinted uncomprehendingly. "Huh? Oh, I get it." He laughed, producing a hyuk-hyuk sound not unlike that of Goofy, the cartoon dog. "Dyke talk, huh? Well, I bet I could learn somethin'."

"No doubt you could," Max stated. "Pity you're not invited."

It took him a moment longer than it should have to realize he was being brushed off, and then he slunk away like a dog who's been caught peeing on the new carpet.

"That was impressive," I gushed. "I don't think I've ever seen your frosty goddess persona before."

She grinned, back to her regular self. "Well, it comes in handy sometimes. It just pisses me off, you know, how if a guy sees two women sitting together, he just assumes they're in need of male company. Because, after all, women aren't interested in each other; they're interested in men." She shook her head. "Pisses me off."

"I know what you mean. There seems to be this innate assumption by men that they're just completely fascinating. Like that guy in my class, Grady Combs, he just rants on in class like the only reason we meet twice a week is so we can hear his latest opinions. And then after class is over, he's always in my face, telling me some allegedly funny thing that some right-wing, loony talk-show host said on the radio the other day, or saying that he wants to keep in touch after he's out of my class in case he ever needs to ask me for a recommendation. I'm thinking, here's a recommendation for you, Grady: Shut up!"

Max laughed. "My mamaw used to say, 'Men's fools, Maxie, and full of talk. But if you let one of 'em talk your drawers down around your ankles, then you're a bigger fool than they is.' " She grinned. "I guess you could say I listened to my mamaw a little too well."

"That sounds like something my Nanny would say."

"That's something I really like about you," Max said, pouring the remains of the pitcher and signaling the bartender for another. "You've got a nanny, I've got a mamaw, we both grew up in the middle of nowhere. It's common ground, you know? Anna, she grew up in the suburbs, and ritzy suburbs at that. Sometimes it makes it hard to, you know, relate. I mean, I grew up in a fucking trailer park, you know?"

The second pitcher arrived, and I looked at it with some trepidation. I was already pretty toasty.

"It's not that I envy Anna really," Max was saying. "Her parents are cold, bigoted assholes who only wanted a daughter so they could marry her off in a big, showy white wedding. And while I would be more than happy to play the groom in that little tableau, I don't think that's what they have in mind. Anna's life compared to my life is like some cliché country song. She grew up rich, but her family never showed her any love. And me, I was always confident I was loved, even though sometimes we ate nothing but oatmeal twice a day because it was the only food in the house." She rolled her eyes self-deprecatingly. "Yep, we were happy in our trailer there on Walton's Mountain."

"Has Anna met your family?"

"Oh, yeah, they treat her like a daughter-in-law. Mother and Daddy have always said, 'Well, if you like girls I reckon that's your business.' And it's never been a problem. Anna's rich, supposedly educated father, on the other hand, thinks homosexuality is a capital offense."

"Well, you can't blame Anna for not coming out to him."

"Hell, no. I mean, she's willing to live in a crappy little rental house in a poor neighborhood with me and pay her own way through school to be independent of those people. You've got to admire that — and I do." She grinned. "Of course, sometimes, the rich girl/poor girl differences do come up, and when they do, they drive me up the fucking wall."

"Like what?"

"Oh, it's just stupid shit, mostly. Like sometimes, she'll eat half an apple, decide she doesn't want the rest, and then throw it away. Or she'll drink a few sips of a Coke and then just leave it to go flat. It drives me nuts because when I see food, I see money, you know. So I'll finish her Coke whether I'm thirsty or not. I even fish her apples out of the garbage and wash them off and eat them. I just can't stand to see food go to waste. Which makes her think I'm a neurotic freak, and, well, she's probably right."

To my amazement, we had polished off the second pitcher. "If you even mention more beer, I'm gonna spew."

"I know what you mean. The phrase *drunk and bloated* does kind of pop to mind. I will play you one more game of pinball, though."

We staggered over to the pinball machine. This time, we were drunk, so we both sucked. To my amazement, I won. "I see what the trick is now," I said. "I should never play you when I'm sober."

We walked back to my apartment with our arms

around each other, partly out of affection and partly because we needed help standing up.

When we stumbled into the living room, Oscar Wildcat squinted up at us disapprovingly.

"That's quite a judgmental look on your cat's face," Max said.

I flopped down on the futon and scratched Oscar's ears. "I'm sure he's thinking that if Mommy went to the vet and got fixed, she wouldn't feel the need to stay out carousing half the night." I leaned my head back. "Wow, you know, when you stop walking, the beer stops sloshing in your stomach." I suddenly remembered my manners. "Uh, do you want a cup of tea or anything?"

"No more liquid of any type, thanks. As a matter of fact, I'm off to get rid of some now."

She disappeared into the bathroom, and I leaned back against the wall, disinterestedly observing the rolling motion the room had taken on. No doubt about it, I couldn't hold my beer like I used to. I could still hold a conversation, but when alone, I floated away into the la-la land of intoxication.

Max plopped down on the futon beside me. I hadn't even heard her come in the room.

"Jess, there's absolutely no way I can drive myself home."

"S'OK. You can stay."

"I can call a cab or something."

"Stay. It's no problem. If I have to wake up in the morning feeling like shit, at least I won't have to do it alone."

Unfolding the futon, we each fell once and used at least three profanities. "Is it just me, or are we like Lucy and Ethel here?" Max laughed.

She borrowed a T-shirt and boxers and changed in the bathroom while I changed in the living room. After I turned out the light, I lay on the futon, and she lay on the floor beside it. "Max?"

"Yeah?"

"I don't think I can sleep with you curled up on the floor like a faithful spaniel."

"I just didn't want you to think —"

"I'm not thinking. I'm drunk. Get in bed. There's plenty of room."

Minutes passed in a drunken blur, then, "Sarah Reed, huh?"

I turned to face Max. "What about her?"

"She was your first and only, right? Sarah Reed?"

"Mm-hmm."

"I wonder . . ."

"What?"

"Never mind."

"No, tell me."

"I wonder . . . how things would have been different if it had been me."

"With Sarah?"

"No. With you, Jess. With you."

I don't know who was responsible for the kiss; I don't know if one person can be held responsible for a kiss that is reciprocated. All I know is that there was a kiss and then another, and that the futon was rolling like a raft on the ocean, and that Max, whom I had hero-worshiped all through college, was unbuttoning my pajama top and whispering that I was beautiful and why hadn't she known it sooner, and oh it had been so long since a woman touched me, not since Sarah, and even though I knew what Max and I were doing was dangerous and that the little raft we were floating on would run aground by morning, when I opened my mouth, the only word that would come out was *yes*.

Blinding rays of sunlight stabbed my eyes. My mouth was entirely devoid of saliva, my head was throbbing, and Max was beside me. I peeked under the covers to confirm my suspicion: yep, naked. What I had hoped had been an erotic dream had turned into a neurotic reality.

"Max?" I touched her shoulder gingerly, as if I was afraid of leaving telltale fingerprints.

"Anna?" she whispered in her sleep.

I buried my face in my pillow. Waves of guilt washed over me like the waves of drunkenness from the night before. I thought of confiding in Anna over lunch, of laughing with her at the vet's office, of her earnest desire that I not be alone. Well, I wasn't alone now. I was with her lover, while she was off nursing her sick grandmother, no less. All this time loving Sarah, I had been congratulating myself that I was the faithful one, the one capable of loyalty and commitment, and here I was, just like the other legions of human beings, destroying the people I loved because my actions sprang solely from my own hormones and insecurities.

"Max?"

"Huh?" She opened her eyes and looked disoriented for a moment, then opened her eyes wider. "Oh, shit."

I handed her her clothes. She pulled on her shirt quickly and slipped on her underwear and jeans under the covers.

"Uh, why don't I make us a cup of tea?"

119

"Yeah, OK." When I came back from the kitchen, Max had already folded the futon back into sofa position, so everything was prim and proper. She accepted the mug of tea, being careful not to touch me as she did so. She looked up at me with wet, red eyes. "You know I love Anna, don't you?"

I erupted in a fit of nervous laughter. "Max, just 'cause I'm a li'l ol' country gal don't mean I think you have to marry me 'cause you had your way with me. I don't think there's such a thing as a lesbian shotgun wedding, is there?" Max didn't crack a smile, so I tried to reign in my hysteria. "I know you love Anna. What happened last night wasn't planned . . . it just happened."

"I don't know what I'm gonna tell her, Jess. I mean, last night was like going back in time. Like we were doing what we should've done back at Hamilton, but never did because we were both working under the faulty assumption that you were straight. But what you and I did last night didn't make us go back in time any more than your obsessing over your one night with Sarah is going to make her go back to what she used to have with you." She wiped her eyes, and it dawned on me that I had never seen Max cry before. "Of course, I do think that if your first time had been with me instead of Sarah, you'd be a lot less fucked up than you are now. Because, unlike Sarah, I wouldn't be denying I was a dyke, and you and I would still be friends."

"And now?"

"Now what?"

"Are we still friends?"

"I can't blame you for a mutual fuck-up. Not that I didn't enjoy last night, but I generally prefer an

120

afterglow to an aftermath." She set down her mug. "We're both agreed that nothing like this is ever gonna happen again, right?"

"Right."

"Then maybe the best thing is if I just don't tell Anna."

"It's your relationship, Max. I'll go along with whatever you say." I wiped away a tear that was sliding down my cheek. "I just don't know how I'm gonna deal with her, though. I feel so guilty; I know I'll act guilty, too."

"Well, you're going home for Thanksgiving break next week, right?"

"Yeah." I shuddered. The thought of dealing with my family when my life was in such turmoil wasn't exactly comforting.

"Well, maybe getting away for a few days will help. Maybe some geographical distance will build some emotional distance." She sighed. "Jess, there's something else we need to talk about. I was going to tell you last night, but we got . . . distracted."

"Yeah?"

"It's about Sarah." She looked up, registering the fear in my eyes. "When she gives you that whole line about being totally straight, and how what happened with you was something that never happened before, that's bullshit."

My stomach clenched. "What do you mean?"

"I slept with her before you did, Jess. Her sophomore year."

I felt numb, like someone had just cut off my arm, and my body had gone into shock. The words spilled out before I could think about them. "I don't believe you."

"Why? Because Sarah's too pure and perfect to be defiled by the likes of me? Jesus, I don't understand how you can keep on idealizing someone who won't even acknowledge your existence. She shits potpourri, to hear you talk."

"Why didn't you say something that night when I first told you about her and me? I mean, you acted so shocked."

"I was shocked. I didn't think she'd ever sleep with another woman. She acted like I was some twisted creature of the night after we did it. It was like we were acting out one of those old lesbian pulp novels, where the beautiful but fiendish lesbian seduces the naive straight girl."

I had pulled my knees against my chest, hugging myself into a tight little ball. But no matter how small I made myself, it wasn't as small as I felt. "How . . . how did it happen?" It was excruciating — I didn't want to know, but I had to know.

"We had a speech class together. Everybody was supposed to pair up to do debates. I, naturally, wanted my topic to be gay rights, and everybody was too scared to debate me, particularly on that issue. Finally Sarah said she'd be my partner, which was, I guess, pretty courageous for such a quiet little straight girl. So we started doing research together, and I even helped her with her *con* argument so it didn't sound quite so reactionary.

"So anyway, the night before the debate we were in my room working on the finishing touches, and she hits me with this zinger of a pickup line. She looks at me with those guileless blue eyes and says, 'Are you really a lesbian?' I tell her it would be a stupid thing to fake, seeing as how it got me treated like shit by most of my fellow students. And she kind of flutters her eyelashes and says, 'I've always wondered what two women do together.' So, as they say, one thing led to another, and I proceeded to show her."

"She wasn't even drunk?"

"Nope, but the next day in debate class her antigay argument was particularly heated, and every time I tried to approach her after that, she looked at me like I was Dracula's daughter."

I couldn't speak. I thought I had known Sarah as well as I had known myself. Now I knew no one, nothing.

Max rose. "Look, I'm sorry, OK? But I thought you needed to know." She headed toward the door. "I'm gonna go now, OK?"

"OK." I knew I should get up, too, but I couldn't.

"Are you gonna be all right?"

"Yeah," I mumbled, not believing it. "I've got to go to school in a few minutes." The thought of walking through a normal workday, even as my life lay in broken shards around my feet, was laughable.

"Um, I think it would be a good idea if we kind of stayed away from each other for the next week or so," Max said. "Let things settle."

I didn't even look up. "Sure. Whatever."

Moments later, I stood in the shower and sobbed, the tears that poured from my eyes as hot as the water that pounded my trembling shoulders.

Chapter 14

I headed home the Wednesday before Thanksgiving, with a mewing Oscar Wildcat in the passenger seat and three garbage bags of dirty laundry in the back. As soon as I hit the interstate, Oscar leaped up onto the dashboard, peered through the windshield, and experienced a full-blown freakout.

"Meee-yew!" he wailed as he caught sight of a rapidly approaching exit sign. He scuttled across the dashboard and stared at me with dilated pupils. His fur was bristling, his claws out for attack. "Meee-yew!" he repeated, as if to say, "Don't you understand? This thing we're in is moving! We're going to fucking die here!"

I plucked him off the dashboard and set him back down on the passenger seat. "It's OK, Oscar. I'm in control here."

He regarded me with narrowed eyes, looking like he didn't believe me any more than I did.

In fact, the car was the only thing I felt like I was in control of. I hadn't talked to Max since the morning after our drunken debacle. I didn't even know if Anna was back in town. The footage of Max and Sarah kept playing over and over in my mind like a film loop to feed my masochism, and the whole time, I kept trying to find a way to convince myself that Max was the seducer, and Sarah the innocent. But even if I could convince myself of that, how could I rationalize Sarah treating me like a perverted predator?

Once I could say that at least I had my friends, but now I had lost Max and Anna, lost track of Amanda and B. J. I was avoiding Christopher so I wouldn't feel compelled to tell him how fucked up my life was. And I had lied to Michelle, a potential friend, fucking things up so badly that there was probably no potential left.

No matter how long I stayed gone or how turbulent my life became, the landscape of Morgan, Kentucky, stayed the same. As I drove down Main Street, there was the Hardee's, the opening of which was a major source of excitement my fifth-grade year. A little farther down the block was Kathy's Kut 'n

Kurl, where I once got such a frizzy perm that my junior high classmates told me I looked like I had stuck my finger in a light socket. And there, at the end of the street, presiding over all the town's activities, stood the yellow-brick, white-columned Morgan First Baptist Church. I hadn't darkened the door of the church in nearly ten years, but they still sent me generic, typed birthday postcards that always read, "Wishing you a joyous birthday and a year in which you grow in Christ's love — from Brother Ralph and all your friends at Morgan First Baptist Church." That's the thing about small-town churches; once they've got hold of you, they're about as likely to let go as a snapping turtle.

I turned left at the end of the street, my little car complaining as it climbed the steep hill that led to my neighborhood. I drove past the Church of God Mountain Assembly, made a left at the Jiffy Sack, and arrived at a street filled with nearly identical three-bedroom, ranch-style houses sitting on nearly identical half-acre plots of land. I pulled into the driveway of the third house on the right and then sat in the parked car for a few seconds telling myself, I am ready for this, everything will be fine.

Mom had hung a bunch of Indian corn on the door, along with a huge paper turkey with puffy tissue paper tail feathers. She always had gone a little nuts with the holiday decorations. I had no doubt that tomorrow she'd have Dad teetering on the roof, hanging Christmas lights. With Oscar squirming in my arms, I rang the doorbell.

When the door opened, the sagey smell of Thanksgiving cooking filled my nose. "Hello, stranger!"

"Hi, Mom."

Mom was wearing an orange sweater decorated with a pattern of autumn leaves. Her hair, which never stayed the same color for long, was golden brown with blond highlights.

"And this must be Oscar," she crooned, giving his velvety nose a quick stroke. One of the few things I had told my mother of late was that I had a cat. "Oscar, why don't you get on down so I can give my daughter a hug?"

I set Oscar down on the light blue carpet and hugged my mom. She pulled away, as she always did, with her arms still touching my shoulders, so she could look at me. "You look great, Jessie. So thin. Have you been dieting?"

Yeah, Mom. It's called the Unrequited Love Diet. "Not really."

"Can you tell I've lost some?" She pivoted in front of me like a fashion model. "I've been going to the Weight Watchers group that meets over at the college."

"Yeah, you look great." Mom was one of those women who spends her life gaining and losing the same ten pounds. "Where's Dad?"

"He went over to pick up your nanny and papaw. You want to come into the kitchen with me? I need to check the dressing."

"Sure, just let me go see Molly first."

"She's on the couch in the den. She doesn't move from that spot much."

Molly was the family cat, now twelve years old. An enormous agouti tabby, she had never been much for physical activity. Now, as an elderly kitty, she had made the den couch the throne from which she surveyed her subjects like an aged but still stately queen. I knelt down and scratched her head. She didn't open her eyes, but craned her neck so her chin could receive some attention.

Oscar was rubbing against my ankle jealously. "Mew!" he insisted. Molly opened one eye, glanced down at Oscar with utter disdain, and then closed her eye again.

The living room door swung open. "Where's my punkin?"

"In here, Dad." My dad looked as much like a junior-high math teacher as is physically possible — glasses, receding hairline, too many pens in his shirt pocket. Even though he was on break from school, he still had chalk on his pants. He gave me a quick hug, then said, "I'll be right back. I've got to bring in Papaw's oxygen tanks."

Until that moment, I hadn't noticed that Nanny and Papaw were standing in the doorway. I had seen them over the summer, and yet I was still surprised by how old they looked. Papaw had changed; he was thin to the point of fragility, shoulders stooped, cheeks sunken. "Hey, buddy," he said, flashing me a still-brilliant, denture-filled smile. "Wanna chaw of tobacca?"

It was our running gag — a gag that had been running since I was five years old. "I believe I'll pass." As I stood beside him, I noticed that he was now shorter than I was. He probably weighed less, too. I draped my arm around his shoulders. So frail.

Nanny was standing behind him, clutching her handbag to her chest as if someone might try to steal it. I wrapped my arm around her in a half hug. "How're you doing, Nanny?"

She looked me up and down, her eyes narrowed.

"When I was growin' up, we always said people that run around with holes in their britches was trashy."

I looked down at my favorite holey-kneed Levi's, which were worn down until the denim was as soft and thin as Kleenex. Trashy or not, I'd wear them 'til they disintegrated around my ankles. "Nice to see you, too, Nanny."

Mom only allowed us to use the dining room on holidays. The two front rooms of the house, the immaculate dining room and living room, were strictly for show. Everyday dining took place in the kitchen, and everyday living took place in the den. As a teenager, I used to call the living room/dining room combo "the shrine."

Now we were all seated at the table in the shrine, a table loaded down with turkey, dressing, gravy, mashed sweet potatoes topped with miniature marshmallows, green bean casserole topped with Durkee french-fried onion rings (for holiday meals, all vegetables were heavily accessorized), dinner rolls, cranberry Jell-O salad, and the cornbread that Nanny had brought.

According to Nanny, a meal wasn't a meal without cornbread. She had also brought a meatloaf. She refused to eat turkey because, as I had heard her say a thousand times, "I ain't gonna eat no animal that ain't got sense enough to come in out of the rain."

I wondered what the staunchly vegetarian Jennifer would think of the idea of not eating an animal because it was too stupid to deserve to be eaten.

We all helped ourselves to the food, Papaw not putting more than a teaspoon of anything on his plate and Nanny taking nothing but meatloaf and cornbread and Jell-O. She always regarded her daughter's cooking with suspicion, as if Mom might try to poison her as revenge for a difficult adolescence.

"So," Nanny said, "you got a feller yet?"

"Nope," I said, stuffing a forkful of marshmallows into my mouth as an excuse to say nothing else.

"Mother," Mom said, swooping to my rescue, "I'm sure Jessie's too busy with school to have time for a boyfriend."

Nanny wagged a hunk of cornbread at me. "I've never seen somebody go to school so long in all my life."

Papaw winked at me. "That's 'cause she's got her papaw's smarts, ain't that right, buddy?"

"Yep," I said, then desperate to shift the focus of the conversation, I asked, "Mom, is there any good gossip over at the college?"

"Not really. Of course, after the big scandal last spring, any gossip would pale by comparison."

"What scandal?"

"I can't believe I didn't tell you about it," Mom said, peeling the skin off a piece of turkey breast to save calories. "This girl they hired over in the English department, Pritchard I think her name was, gave a big speech in the auditorium and ended it by telling everybody she was a lesbian."

Until that moment, I hadn't known it was physically possible to choke on Jell-O. I took a quick swig of tea and said, "Really? What happened to her?"

Mom leaned over conspiratorially. "Well, all h-e-double-l broke loose, as you can imagine. She was pretty much fired on the spot, and they brought in a part-time person to take over her classes. I thought it was kind of a shame. I met her once, and she seemed like a nice girl. Long hair, trim figure, nice clothes. You'd never know she was a lesbian to look at her."

I shifted uncomfortably in my seat, thinking my mom wasn't exactly batting a thousand at the spot-the-lesbian game anyway.

I was about to change the subject to football, to the weather, to anything, when Nanny looked up from her meatloaf and asked, "What's a lesbian?"

Papaw leaned toward her and said, in the learned tone Sigmund Freud might have used if he had possessed a Southeastern Kentucky accent, "A lesbian is a woman who's . . . funny."

Nanny looked justifiably puzzled. "Funny how?"

"You know," Papaw said, "funny that way."

Dad, who hates an imprecise definition more than Mr. Webster probably did, set down his fork and gently explained, "Nanny, a lesbian is a woman who likes other women — who sleeps with other women."

"Well, I don't see nothin' wrong with that," Nanny said. "Girls sleep in the same bed together all the time. Why, when I was a girl I used to sleep with my sister Beulah and my cousin Myrtle, and if that makes me a lesbian, well, I don't think that's anything to be ashamed of!"

Look out, everybody, I thought, Nanny's coming out of the closet! I started laughing so hard I couldn't get my breath.

Nanny glared at me and said, "What are you laughin' at, young'n?" which, of course, just made me laugh harder.

Papaw looked solemnly down at his plate and muttered, "Arlene, you ain't no lesbian."

"So," my mom chirped brightly, "who's ready for pumpkin pie?"

* * * * *

As I lay in bed Thanksgiving night, I marveled at
my ability to love my family despite their ability to
drive me crazy. Mom's weight obsession, Dad's
obliviousness, Papaw's passivity, Nanny's crotchetiness
— all of these characteristics had driven me up the
wall at one time or another.

I had even dreaded this visit, afraid of squirming
in the knowledge of my secret life. And I did squirm
at the dinner table, for a while. But it had ended
with me laughing and eating a huge slab of pumpkin
pie.

Home wasn't a safe haven because of its Norman
Rockwellian perfection; it was just safer than the big,
bad world because the annoyances I encounter at
home are always the same ones I've been dealing with
all my life. And when life is spinning out of control,
there's something to be said for annoyances that are
predictable.

My problems back in Louisville were new, scary
ones. I looked around my old room. The dresser was
still cluttered with all the meaningless little awards
and trophies I'd won in high school, and the walls
were still decorated with posters of James Dean and
David Bowie looking like androgynous dykes. The
bookshelves were lined with the books I'd loved
during my adolescence, *Jane Eyre*, *Wuthering Heights*,
Rebecca — all those classic "girl books" populated by
stone mansions and dark secrets. I fantasized briefly
about never leaving this room, this site of my

adolescent self-absorption, about only leaving my narrow, chenille-covered bed to retrieve a beloved book off the shelf.

But my life wasn't in Morgan, not even in the haven of my girlhood room — it never had been, really. Throughout junior high and high school, I spent most of my hours dreaming about that magical time when I would live Somewhere Else and do Something Else.

If my life were a verb tense, it would be future perfect. My mind was always fixated on a flawless future, which often blinded me to events that were going on in front of my nose. If I hadn't been so busy living in that future perfect time when Sarah would leave Mike and come back to me, maybe I wouldn't have let myself drunkenly fall into bed with Max, endangering Max and Anna's real, living, breathing relationship. I was like some poor pedestrian who was so busy looking at the cars in the distance that she didn't notice the approaching eighteen-wheeler which was about to turn her into roadkill.

My life in Louisville was a mess, but it was my mess. Tomorrow morning I would kiss my parents good-bye and head back into my own little vortex of chaos. It was time to start living life in the present tense.

Chapter 15

The 'Madness' of Victorian Gender Roles:
Charlotte Perkins Gilman's 'The Yellow Wallpaper'

I frowned at the glowing title on the computer
screen. Since returning from Morgan, I had thrown
myself into my schoolwork. I had no choice, really. I
had two final papers due in two weeks, and while I
did want to straighten out my personal life, I didn't
want to flunk out of school in the process.

The doorbell rang. I saved my title, dumped Oscar

off my lap, and looked through the door's peephole. It was Anna.

I couldn't have been more terrified if it had been a police officer brandishing a gun and a warrant for my arrest. Just act natural, I told myself, wondering why stressful moments can transform reasonably intelligent people into B-movie characters. As I opened the door, I felt the emotion that goes with living life in the present tense — unadulterated quivering terror. "Hey, Anna. Come on in."

"Thanks."

Was it my imagination, or were her eyes red and puffy? I was so paranoid I was finding it difficult to be objective. "Uh, where's Max?" I could've ripped my tongue out the second I said it. Jesus, why didn't I just say, "Where's your girlfriend, with whom I had a drunken sexual encounter?"

"Her brother's in town. They went to a movie." Her mirthlessness was definitely not a product of my imagination. "You mind if I sit down?"

"Of course not." And there she sat, right on the futon where Max and I had wallowed naked. God, I wished I was having a root canal, being drawn and quartered, anything other than looking into the eyes of a friend I had wounded.

"How's your grandma?"

"Recovering nicely, thanks." Her tone was falsely cordial.

"Um, can I get you something?" Beer, coffee, a Louisville Slugger to bludgeon me?

"A beer'd be good."

I got us each one. I handed her the bottle and sat down across from her on the floor. I couldn't bring myself to sit on the futon.

She knocked back a third of the bottle, then said, "I may not be able to talk about James Joyce or Faulkner like you and Maxie can, but I know some things." She brushed away a tear that was sliding down her cheek. "I know what it means when a girlfriend gets too nice all of a sudden, treating me like a needy child instead of a grown woman. And I know what it means when a girlfriend gets all jumpy when a certain friend's name comes up. I'm not stupid, Jess." Her voice was dead, empty.

"I never said you were." Desperate for a nervous gesture, I peeled the label off my beer bottle. "What happened . . . wasn't about deceiving you. It was about being drunk and stupid and thoughtless." Oscar had settled on my lap, but he moved away in irritation when my tears kept plopping on his head. "Anna, I can promise you it'll never happen again, but I don't guess a promise coming from me means much right now."

"No, it doesn't."

"If you want, I'll just stay the hell away from you and Max." Then it occurred to me. "You and Max are still together?"

Her lips stretched in a near smile, but failed to turn up at the corners, like the humorless grin of a death's head. "Yeah, we're together. Our relationship isn't exactly at its healthiest. I make her feel guilty; she lets me." She drained her beer. "We'll get past it eventually. I love her, so we'll get past it." She tried to look me in the eye, but I turned away, sobbing. "I don't know what to do about you, Jess."

My words came out in waves with my sobs. "I don't know either. I'll do whatever you say. If you want me to stay away from y'all, I'll do it. If you want to kill me, I totally understand."

She half smiled. "I did think about killing you there at first. But I figured the last thing the world needs is another true-crime story about killer lesbians."

"Well, thanks for granting me a stay of execution."

"No problem, this time." She caught my eye and willed me not to look away. "But if you ever touch Maxie again in anything other than a chaste, sisterly way, I will change my mind."

"I understand." She rose to leave with the unanswered question still hanging in the air: Is this the end of our friendship? But all that would come out of my mouth was, "So ... ?"

"So?"

"So ... so previous to my big fuck-up, you and Max were my best friends here. I know I damaged our friendship, but is there still a friendship left?"

She ran a finger under her eyes. "I'll tell you what. I need some time to get my shit together ... for Maxie and me to get our shit together. Give us a week, then call us. We'll see what happens."

"Oh, Anna, I'm so sorry about all this." I moved to hug her, but she stiffened.

"I'm not ready to hug, Jess."

"OK." I wanted to at least touch her with words. "Uh, Anna — I just want to say that if the situation had been reversed, if it had been you and I alone together, getting drunk, the same thing could've happened."

"No." Her manner was dignified, almost regal. "I would never be unfaithful to Maxie."

And with that, she was gone.

My heart and guts felt like a wadded-up piece of discarded tissue paper. So this was how it felt to live in the present. "Press any key to continue," the glowing computer screen mocked.

I went to the kitchen and got another beer for me and a Pounce treat for Oscar. I had to admit, underneath this wrung-out, sucked-dry feeling, there was relief. The ugly scene was over, and I was still breathing. The walls hadn't come tumbling down, and the beer tasted damned good.

Maybe there was something to this honesty thing. Maybe Sarah should try it. Not a chance. If you're going to be honest with someone else, you've got to be honest with yourself first.

Of course, I shouldn't be giving myself any medals yet either. Even before the night with Max, there had been more deception — someone I had deceived out of my own misguided sense of self-protection. I opened my closet door — not in the metaphorical sense — and took out my denim jacket. There, in the right-hand pocket, on the back of a business card for the Starlite, was Michelle's number.

Chapter 16

Michelle had asked me to meet her for a walk in Cave Hill Cemetery. Walking in a graveyard on a cold, gray day with dead leaves crunching underfoot seemed like an odd way to bring a friendship to life, but I had agreed anyway.

"Great," she had said. "I'll meet you in front of the Peaslee Sphinx."

"The what?"

"The Peaslee Sphinx. Trust me. You'll know it when you see it."

She was right. Beyond the high gates of Cave Hill,

I found Michelle, standing beside a huge stone slab on which the name *Peaslee* had been carved in neat block letters. Perched on top of the slab was a carved Sphinx a little larger than a Great Dane. "Hey, girl," she said (Michelle, not the Sphinx).

"Well, damned if it isn't the Sphinx." I looked up at the Sphinx's cold stone eyes, then down to Michelle's warm brown ones. "Tell me a riddle."

Michelle laughed. "OK, but if you don't answer it, I'll have to eat you up." Her eyes twinkled. "What do you call a troop of well-armed lesbians?"

This joke had been going around like a bad case of the flu. Ralph in the office had already told it to me twice. "Militia Etheridge."

"Damn, you got it right. And you were looking so tasty, too." She grinned. "Well, you answered the Riddle of the Sphinx. I guess all that's left for you to do is kill your father and marry your mother."

"Which, if you listen to the psychobabble, is all we dykes want to do anyway." I was enjoying the banter and knew I could keep it up all afternoon without ever getting around to telling Michelle the truth. What was it Circe had said on our date — that I used my humor as a way to hide my fears?

Michelle laughed again. Even if I did use humor as a defense mechanism, it was good to hear her laugh. "So you want the tour?"

"I'd love it." We started walking.

"I hope you didn't think I was weird for asking you to meet me here, but I really love this place."

"Well, it did seem a little . . . unorthodox at first, but now that I'm here, I understand." I watched swans circling elegantly in the pond below us. "It's really beautiful."

"Yeah, it is beautiful, and it's fascinating, too — all these monuments people have built for themselves, the way people want to be remembered. The irony of it gets me. All these majestic monuments, and the people here are just as dead as the people buried in potter's field."

"Yeah, it's like that Shelley poem, 'Ozymandias,' where there's this crumbling statue in the desert with the inscription, 'I am Ozymandias, King of Kings —' "

" 'Look on my works, ye mighty, and despair,' " Michelle finished. "Yeah, this place has always made me think of that poem, too." She walked over to a life-size statue of a man in a tuxedo. "But still, you've gotta give these people some credit for going out in style." She draped her arm around the statue's shoulder. "This guy was a magician."

Upon closer inspection, I saw that the figure was indeed that of a magician. His face was old and kind, and his hand was outstretched, ready to be shaken. "Hey, you know what'd be cool?" I said. "If shaking the statue's hand triggered an automated hand to rise up out of the grave and grab people's ankles."

Michelle laughed. "And imagine how many more cemetery plots they'd sell, what with all the heart attacks. There's one more thing I want to show you, but it's kind of far away. Are you up for the walk?"

"Sure."

She took my hand. Involuntarily, I glanced around to see if anybody was looking.

"What — you think we're gonna get gay-bashed in the cemetery?"

I was being paranoid, I guess. "No, it's not that —"

"We can always tell people we're sisters." She

looked at our hands. "Well, beneath the skin, anyway."

I laughed, then stopped when Michelle dropped my hand suddenly.

"Shit," she muttered. "I wasn't thinking."

"What do you mean?"

"I forgot about you and Sarah for a minute, you know, when I was holding your hand. I'm sorry. I wasn't making a move on you or anything; I'm just a touchy person."

"Um, actually, I need to talk to you about Sarah."

"What — did you break up or something?"

I stopped walking and leaned against a tree for support. If my confession made Michelle mad enough to kill me, at least I was in the right place. "No, we didn't break up. We were never together. I lied to you, Michelle. I'm sorry."

"Look, Jess, if you didn't want to go out with me, you could've just said so. You didn't have to make up some nonexistent person —"

She was walking fast, so fast I had to half run to keep up with her. "Sarah isn't nonexistent. She was my college roommate. We slept together once. I loved her, but ... she's straight." My words were coming in gasps, as I galumphed along to stay in Michelle's earshot. "That night at the Starlite ... she had just told me she was getting engaged ... I couldn't open myself up to getting hurt again ... Maybe I was just hoping if I said Sarah and I were together, I could make it true."

Michelle wheeled around. I dug my toes into the dirt to keep from bumping into her. "Did you remember to click your heels together three times when you said it?"

"I know it was stupid and hurtful, but people who are hurting do stupid, hurtful things. Sarah was my first, and at the time, I thought I was her first, too. Please don't hate me, Michelle."

Now we were walking at a normal pace, past granite angels and marble mausoleums. Finally, Michelle said, "I'm in no position to hate you, Jess. As you may recall, I've had my own straight-girl soap opera going on."

"Yeah." I heard the relief in my voice. "What's the status of the Jill thing anyway?"

"Well, you can stick a fork in it, honey, because it's done."

"Really?"

"Yeah, not that I had the ovaries to finish it myself, mind you. It kind of got ended for us. Rick came back early from a conference one night and caught us in one of those positions that make it completely ridiculous to say, 'It's not what you think.' Although I think Jill did say it, if I'm not mistaken."

"Shit."

"Shit indeed. You know, Rick's language isn't too poetic when he's angry. I believe what he said was, 'You goddamn dyke, I knew you were fucking that black bitch.' It was one of those moments when the mask really drops, you know?"

"What did you do?"

"I got the hell out of there, is what I did. Picture me with my shirt buttoned wrong, holding my boots in my hand 'cause there was no time to lace them up, running down the sidewalk in this lily-white neighborhood. I'm sure the neighbors thought I'd been caught trying to rob the place."

I stopped to catch my breath. "I shouldn't laugh, but I can't help it."

"I laughed, too, when it was over. Jill called to say she was sorry things had ended that way, but she couldn't afford to lose her husband, blah, blah, blah."

"So I guess getting any more of your poems published in *Barbaric Yawp!* is out of the question."

"Totally out of the question. Whew! No more straight women." She shook her head, humming, "Mm, mm, mm. You know, Jill was the first white woman I'd ever been involved with."

"Will she be the last?"

She grinned mischievously. "Not necessarily." She started walking again. "My favorite gravestone is over here. Let's go look at it."

The gravestone was a simple slab of granite, with no accompanying ornamental sculpture or etchings. The letters that had been carved on it had eroded with time but I could still make out the inscription:

GRACE ADAMSON   MARY ALICE JENKINS
BORN MAY 1822 —   BORN DECEMBER 1825 —
DIED JULY 1893   DIED JANUARY 1894
            BELOVED FRIENDS

"That's amazing," I said, reaching down to trace the epitaph with my fingers.

"Yeah. I found this stone one day when I was just walking around. Since then, I've come to visit Grace and Mary Alice a lot. I talk to them, bring them flowers. Sometimes I sprinkle a little perfume on the grave." She looked at me. "You think I'm crazy?"

Her devotion to this extraordinary place and her desire to share it with me made me overflow with feelings I couldn't find the words for, so I just said, "Not at all."

"Well, let's make a pact, then, right here in front of Grace and Mary Alice." She took both of my hands in hers. "No more straight women."

"No more straight women."

We sealed our pact with a kiss. Even though she only held me lightly, I could still feel the strength in her arms in delicious contrast with the softness of her lips. After we kissed, I stood for a moment with my head on Michelle's shoulder. For the first time, I didn't care if anyone was looking.

Chapter 17

On Monday I was in such a good mood that I actually laughed at Fred's jokes. Actually, I wasn't laughing at the jokes directly; I was just using them as socially appropriate moments to let my happiness bubble to the surface. And why wouldn't I be happy? For the first time since moving to Louisville, I was in control of my life. I had finished one of two major papers; I had not alienated my friends despite the fact that I probably deserved to; and I had the closest thing to a real, live girlfriend I had ever had.

That day, in comp, I was scheduled to teach an essay on homophobia on college campuses. I had been quietly dreading the essay all term, particularly given Grady Combs's diatribes on less controversial subjects, but today, I knew I could handle it.

On the way to class, I ran into Christopher. "Wait," he said, squinting at me. "You look vaguely familiar. Have we met?"

"Point taken. I have been a shitty friend lately, but I promise to do better." I gave him a little half hug. "Let's go out and do something this week. I've got tons of stuff to tell you. You remember Michelle from Sanders's party?"

Christopher smiled knowingly. "Oh, so that's why you haven't called me."

"I'll tell you all about it later. I've got to go teach that essay on homophobia."

"Good luck, girlfriend. I taught that thing last week and came out of the classroom feeling like somebody had been kicking me in the stomach for fifty minutes."

"Thanks for the encouragement." I was determined not to let Christopher bring me down. Surely the class discussion couldn't be that bad.

It was. It's amazing how most racists at least feel a need to disguise their prejudice in the classroom because of the nonwhite faces present, yet homophobes have no qualms about spewing their venom wherever they are, working under the assumption that there could never be any of "those people" in such a "normal" setting. This is the mistake Grady Combs made.

"Now I don't do this, mind you," he brayed. "But

if I wanted to go into the men's room and write 'Faggots, go home' on the wall, then that's my right and nobody has the right to stop me."

I was just about to question the idea of vandalism as a God-given right when Mark, the quiet blond boy who had set off my gaydar since the first day of class, spoke up for the first time all term. "But," he said, "don't I have the right to go to the bathroom without reading something personally offensive to me? When you write 'Faggots, go home,' you're telling me to go home when I have a right to be here and get an education just like everybody else."

Grady, for once, was silent. I felt I had to back Mark up, to show my appreciation of his bravery. "Yes," I said, "let's bear in mind that gays and lesbians make up at least 10 percent of the population. When we speak, let's not assume that everyone in the classroom is heterosexual. Statistically, there are at least two of us here who are not. Now let's go back to the text of the article, shall we?"

Michelle was coming over after she got off work at 11:00. All evening I had been working on my approaches-to-scholarship paper, trying to make use of my time instead of being a lady-in-waiting. But now it was 10:00, and I was soaking in a bubble bath and allowing myself to anticipate Michelle's arrival. What would she say? What would we do? Was the fact that I had wine chilling in the fridge too hokey and self-consciously romantic? Did Michelle even like wine?

My obsessing was interrupted by the ringing phone. The warm water was relaxing, and I didn't want to get out. A thought raced through my mind: It could be Michelle. I ran, naked and dripping, to the phone in the kitchen. "Hello?"

"Miss Hamlin?" The voice, which sounded like a Southern version of Bullwinkle the moose, was instantly recognizable. "This is Grady Combs. How you doin'?"

I hate it when students call me at home, particularly after 10:00 P.M. "Just fine," I lied, grabbing a tiny dish towel with which to inadequately dry myself. "What can I do for you?"

"Well, actually, it's something I wanted to do for you," he drawled. His accent sounded thicker than usual. I wondered if he had been drinking. "My band, Grady and the Diamondtones, we're playin' over at the Cadillac Lounge at the Executive Lodge on Dixie Drive next Friday, and I just wanted you to know that if you want to go, I can get you in for free. I could probably even set you up if you'd like to knock back a coupla cool ones."

I was aghast. I had thought he was going to ask me something about his final paper. "Well, Grady, that's very kind of you, but I think I have a class that night," I lied.

"It's next Friday, Miss Hamlin — not this coming Friday. School'll be out then, so maybe you can make it."

"Uh — maybe."

"Great!" he boomed. "Look, I just wanted to let you know I felt real bad about what happened in class today."

"What do you mean?" The dish towel was soaking wet now, and I was freezing. I had to get off the phone soon.

"Well, when I said that about faggots and everything, you know, I just got so worked up that I forgot that boy Mark in our class is a homosexual. I mean, I knew he was, I can always tell, by the way they walk and everything."

He paused, which probably meant I was supposed to say something, but I had been stricken so mute that if Annie Sullivan had come back from the grave, she wouldn't have been able to make me speak.

"I mean, I still think homosexuality's a perversion and everything, but bein' in the music business, I've known lots of homosexuals and liked 'em as people . . . you know, love the sinner, hate the sin." He paused, and I thought I heard him take a drink of something. "And I got to thinking, I've never heard you say anything about your personal life, you know, about a husband or a boyfriend or a fiancée or anything —"

Oh, shit.

"And I remember you sayin' you was — uh, *were,* sorry — you were from a little-bitty town in Southeastern Kentucky, and I got to thinking if you was a homosexual, it'd be awful hard growin' up there. But I just want you to know I don't care what you are because I like you, Miss Hamlin; I really do. And I don't meet many women I like." He paused, swallowed. "My wife, she left me last year, took my boys with her. Broke my heart, you know, because nobody believes in the family like I do. But I just wanted you to know I think a lot of you, and if you're not a homosexual —"

I found my voice — well, not my usual voice, but a croaky facsimile. "Well, Grady, that's always nice to hear from a student, that you think well of me. But if that's all, I really need to —"

"You know, it's funny," Grady mused, paying no attention to the fact that I was writhing in the steel trap of this conversation. "Like I said, I know a lot of homosexuals from the music scene, and you know, most of the straight guys hate fags and make fun of them and stuff. But I don't know one heterosexual man, myself included, who wouldn't give his best gun and coon dog to see two women go at it!"

My hand spasmed, and the phone receiver crashed to the floor. When I picked it up, Grady was still blathering on, oblivious.

"You know," he said, "I didn't used to be this conservative. I was pretty wild back in the sixties. Yessir, reefer, acid, the whole scene. And the sex! Let me tell you, Miss Hamlin, Grady Combs is no stranger to what a man and two women can do in bed together!"

I looked around frantically for an excuse, any excuse. Finally, out of sheer desperation, I began banging on the wall with my fist. "Listen, Grady," I said, my voice shrill and panicky. "Somebody's knocking on my door. I've gotta go." I slammed down the receiver.

Had I heard what I thought I'd heard? Was it possible that this neo-Nazi demagogue was also some kind of demented dyke daddy? I pictured the young, decadent Grady Combs sprawled on a king-size bed with two stringy-haired sixties chicks and shivered. My skin was covered in goose bumps from standing wet and naked on the cold linoleum. It was bad enough to have to listen to Grady Combs's self-indulgent straight-boy fantasies. Having to do so while naked made me wonder if I was being punished for a crime I had committed in a previous life. Suddenly, I felt the need for another bath.

But there was no time. Michelle would be here any minute. I decided to shake off the Grady Combs call like a dirty dog shakes off muddy water. I had no time to reflect on the Larry Flynt–inspired fantasies of straight white men. I had more important things to obsess over, like what to wear. I wanted to look somewhat sexy for Michelle, but answering the door in my current state seemed too direct.

I had just decided that I didn't own anything sexy and had settled for a sweater and skirt when the doorbell rang.

Michelle still had on her APD uniform under her black leather jacket. The effect was stunning; the sharp lines of the uniform complemented her muscles and contrasted with her womanly curves. She was handsome and beautiful at the same time. "I hope you don't object to a woman in uniform."

"Not at all," I said, meaning it.

"I bought some wine."

"Me, too."

"Great minds think alike."

I just stood there, smiling at her, blocking the doorway.

"So do I get to come in?"

"Oh, yeah. Sorry." I stepped aside and closed the door behind her.

When I turned around, she was standing right in front of me. "Hi," she said and kissed me lightly on the lips. Our second kiss. I hoped that soon there'd be so many I'd lose count.

"Hi," I said back, casting my eyes downward. Making eye contact after a kiss is hard for me.

"So what does a working girl have to do to get a drink around here?"

"I'll be right back."

I returned from the kitchen with coffee mugs full of wine. "It ain't Martha Stewart living, but it's the best I can do."

Michelle grinned. "I hate that skinny white woman anyway."

I settled next to her on the futon.

"Speaking of white women..." she began, looking at me.

"I'm not sure I like that segue. From Martha Stewart to me is quite a leap."

"Granted. I've just been thinking...are you sure you're up for this?"

"Up for what?"

"For dating a black woman."

"Michelle, it doesn't make any difference to me that you're black." As soon as I said it, I realized how I sounded — like that little straight blond freshman in my comp class who said she didn't even notice if a person was black or white. "I guess it does make a difference in a way. But it's a difference I like."

"I just wanted to make sure you know what you're getting yourself into. Because even if it doesn't make a difference to you, it does make a difference to other people."

"Well, fortunately, I don't spend much time around

racist, homophobic bigots." Of course, even as I said it, I thought of my earlier conversation with Grady Combs.

"Jess, rednecks in white hoods aren't the only kind of racists. There's plenty of racism in the gay community."

I shouldn't have been shocked, but I was. I still wanted to believe that gay people were automatically more enlightened than straights. "Well, surely there's not as much —"

"Maybe not, but there's still plenty. That night at the Starlite when I first met you, I was waiting in line for the toilet, and this white dyke sneers at me and says, 'Don't you people have your own bar?' "

"That's harsh."

"And you know that big bar downtown, Expressions?"

"Yeah, I went there once with Max and Anna."

"Well, it's no coincidence that the only black faces you see over there are on the stage. Oh, it's fine to have a black queen or two in the show, dancing and cutting up for the white folks. But when black folks try to come to the club for their own entertainment, let's just say they're made to feel highly unwelcome. Assuming they ever get in the door, they're given the worst seats and the wateriest drinks in the house." She sipped her wine. "Trust me, Jess. I'm not just being paranoid here."

"I believe you."

"And on the flip side are a lot of straight black brothers and sisters, my family members included, who hate queers. And some of my black queer friends will resent that I'm dating a white woman." She shook her head. "I swear, Jess, sometimes it just

154

makes a girl want to get in bed and pull the covers over her head." She looked me in the eye. "So anyway, that's the shit I'm bringing with me into this relationship, if we have one, and that's the kind of shit you and I are going to have to deal with if we ever go past this apartment door. So if it's too much, tell me now before I get too involved, because, Jess, I've got to tell you, I'm really liking you a lot."

I touched her hand. "Well, I'd be pretty reprehensible if I gave up the best person in my life because of what the worst people might say."

Michelle smiled. "Brave girl." She reached over to push my hair out of my face. "I'll tell you what. Right now let's not even think about what's beyond this apartment door."

She took the mug out of my hand and leaned over to kiss me. It was a long, soft kiss — our third kiss, which soon melted into our fourth, our fifth, our sixth, until she was on top of me, struggling to pull my sweater over my head.

"Wait," I said.

She looked up at me with questioning eyes. "Why?"

"Shouldn't we turn the light off?"

"What for?"

"I don't know. Before, it's always been in the dark."

She grinned. "Not this time, honey. This time you're with a woman who wants to see what she's doing."

She shucked off my clothes like she was peeling a banana. I, however, was not as skillful. Weak and trembling with lust, I fumbled with the buttons of her tan workshirt.

"Here, let me help," she said. She stood up and unceremoniously stripped off her shirt, unhooked her bra, and stepped out of her pants. She stood above me, unashamed of her nakedness but seemingly unaware of her beauty.

She was beautiful. I had thought so since the first time I saw her, but some women look even better naked than they do clothed, and Michelle was definitely one of them. Her smooth, caramel-apple skin stretched tight over her arm and thigh muscles, but on the swells of her large breasts, full hips, and rounded belly, it was soft and cushiony. She had the voluptuous curves of a Rubens woman and the sharp muscle definition of a Michelangelo man. I wondered what I had seen in Sarah's frail, birdlike frame, now that I saw this woman of strong muscle and bountiful flesh.

I didn't have time to admire Michelle for long; within seconds of undressing, she was on top of me, her large breasts pressing against my small ones, my pale legs entwining her dark ones.

She took me softly at first, her fingers gentle and teasing, learning my body's rhythms, teaching me that I wanted more. She increased her speed and force gradually, building and building until I called her name and then until I couldn't utter her name and could barely remember my own.

When we stopped to rest, we realized that somehow we had made our way from the futon all the way across the floor to the kitchen door. I laughed. "How did we get over here?"

"Well, you just kept rolling and scooting, rolling and scooting, and you know what Ruth says to Naomi in the Bible: 'Whither thou goest, I will go.' "

"Well, this is certainly an interesting time to start quoting the Bible. Why don't we move back to the futon? This linoleum is getting kind of cold."

She lay back on the futon and smiled and sighed as I explored her loveliness with my hands and mouth.

Afterward, as we lay together, Michelle said, "You can't tell me that Georgia O'Keeffe didn't have sex with women."

"What?" The intensity of our sexual encounter had made me slow on the uptake.

She pointed to the picture on my wall. "Look at that, the way those petals are layered, the opening in the middle. That ain't a flower she was painting." She cocked her head to examine it at a different angle. "She must've had sex with women."

"Either that or she had an unusually close relationship with her hand mirror."

Her laugh was deep and hearty. "You're a crazy woman."

"Can't you imagine her, with one foot up on a chair, holding the mirror in her left hand, painting with her right?"

Michelle put on a serious face. "That's not funny. Georgia O'Keeffe is one of our most significant women artists." But then her mouth turned up at the corners, and soon she was laughing again. "OK, so maybe it's a little funny."

I cuddled up against her. "Michelle?"

"Mm-hm?"

"Will you stay here with me tonight?"

"There's no place I'd rather be."

Chapter 18

Even though I had to get up after only five hours of sleep, I awoke in a fabulous mood. For the first time the woman with whom I had made love and I were able to open our eyes and look at each other and smile — no hangovers, no horror, no regrets.

I tickled Michelle's face with one of her braids. "Go back to sleep. I have to go drop my approaches-to-scholarship paper in my professor's mailbox. I won't be gone an hour."

"Mm," she said, settling back down into her pillow.

"I'll bring us breakfast."

I showered and dressed quickly, grabbed my paper, and walked out into the morning sun. It was one of those sunny winter days, impossibly bright and cold. I hugged myself and smiled. I was so damned perky that if I had been wearing a hat, I would've thrown it up in the air like Mary Tyler Moore.

I dropped my paper off at school and then stopped at the deli near campus to buy bagels. I would tiptoe into the apartment, careful not to wake Michelle, quietly make some tea and slice some fruit, and then serve her breakfast in bed.

But when I got back to my apartment, what I saw just about made me drop my bagels. Michelle was standing in the doorway, dressed in her rumpled APD uniform. Her eyes, which had been so soft and loving last night, were now coals that smoldered with fury. "Look," she said, before I could ask what was wrong. "I don't know if you're into the whole nonmonogamy thing or not. I guess we didn't talk about it because it just never occurred to me that we'd need to."

"Michelle, I'm really confused." I should have known my happiness would be fleeting. This seemingly sensible, wonderful woman apparently turned into a raving lunatic after you slept with her. It was like a bad movie straight people would write about lesbians.

"You're confused?" she snapped. "Look, Jess, were you entertaining another guest before I came over last night? Because if you were, I think I have a right to know."

"Michelle, I have no idea what you're talking about. All I did before you came over was finish my paper."

"Yeah? Well, how do you explain this?" She forced a small rectangle of white paper into my hand.

I looked down at the card, mystified. On it were the words:

Thanks for everything last night,
sorry I was a little drunk.
See you next Friday.
— G.C.

The whole conversation with Grady Combs flooded back into my mind, from his denouncement of homosexuality to his willingness to trade his prized hunting dog and firearm in order to see two women — how had he put it? — "go at it." I glanced over at the coffee table and saw what the card had accompanied: a dozen red roses.

I finally dropped the bagels. I sank to the floor, too, to keep them company. "Oh, Michelle," I cried, "Oh, shit." I caught my breath, and in a rush of disjointed words, told her the tale of Grady Combs.

Michelle listened more and more patiently as it became evident that I wasn't nearly creative enough to make something like this up. When I finished, she rubbed her chin and then announced in a deliberate, almost clinical tone, "I'm going to kill him."

I laughed nervously.

"You think I'm kidding, don't you?" She shook her head. "Before I went to college, I hung out with some tough dykes. Big, scary black butches who'd ram a pool cue up a man's ass just as casually as they'd light up a cigarette. I know where to find those women."

"Oh, I can see it now," I said. "You, a black

160

lesbian, telling the white heterosexual judge and jury that you murdered a white heterosexual man because you didn't like the way he talked to your white girlfriend."

She sighed. "You probably have a point. Damn straight white men anyway. They can treat every woman like their erotic property, and you can't get even with them because they run the fucking world."

I draped my arm around her. "Well, it's kind of a defeatist attitude, but in this case, it's appropriate." I picked up the paper bag. "So how about a bagel?"

Over bagels and tea, Michelle said, "I'm sorry I came at you like I did. I guess the thing with Jill has made me kind of paranoid."

"That's OK." I glanced at the huge vase of roses. "It's not like you didn't have grounds for suspicion."

Michelle eyed the flowers. "I bet that sonuvabitch would just love to cure you of your 'perversion.' "

"Yeah, but he'd get an even bigger charge out of watching you and me in the throes of perverted passion." I licked the cream cheese from my lips. "On second thought, maybe not. He might be too upset by the sight of you defiling my precious white woman-hood."

Michelle laughed. "I'll tell you a secret about those right-wing white boys, Jess. The only place they're for affirmative action is in the bedroom."

"What do you mean?"

"I mean that those racist fuckers always have the hots for black women, at least on a subconscious level. The massa may be respectful and deferential to his lily-white wife in the daytime, but when night comes, he sneaks down to the slave cabin for a little action." Her face lit up suddenly. "You know, I think I may have just talked myself into a hell of a plan for Mr. Grady Combs."

"What do you mean?"

"I mean, there's no hope of bringing a straight, white man to justice in the straight, white world. But if we unknowingly drag Mr. Combs into our world . . ." She laughed maniacally — cutely, but maniacally.

"You're being awfully mysterious."

"I know. I'm still thinking, and I have to make a phone call or two before I know if I can pull it off. So . . . you think your friends Max and Anna and Christopher might derive some pleasure from humiliating a Bible-banging, gay-bashing, G-Gordon-Liddy lover?"

"Sure. What self-respecting queer wouldn't? But we are talking about humiliation here, right? Not death or dismemberment?"

"However tempting, no. I tell you what. Why don't you get in touch with your friends and see if they can come over to my place for dinner tomorrow night? And there, if all goes well, I will reveal my secret weapon."

"You're being mysterious again."

"I know."

"You're sexy when you're mysterious."

She smiled. "I know."

We kissed, a long, deep kiss.

"Keep that up, honey, and I may never leave this apartment."

"OK by me."

"Me, too. Unfortunately, I've got a parrot at home who's probably fresh out of birdseed."

"I didn't know you had a bird."

"There's a lot you don't know about me."

I looked over at the roses, which had an unfortunate tendency to dominate the room. "I wish I knew what to do with those flowers. I don't want to keep them, but it seems a shame to throw them away. It's not the roses' fault that they were bought by an asshole."

Michelle regarded the bouquet for a moment, then said, "I think I have an idea."

That afternoon, just before Michelle had to go to work, we met in Cave Hill Cemetery and scattered the roses, one by one, over Grace and Mary Alice's grave.

Chapter 19

Michelle busied around her kitchen, stirring the pot of navy-bean soup, measuring out the cornmeal, all the while with Miss Celie the gray parrot sitting on a shoulder like a pirate's first mate. Max, Anna, Christopher, and I sipped our beers at the kitchen table beneath a poster of Billie Holiday.

"You and Jess are gonna have some interesting pet dynamics going on, if the two of you move in together," Max observed.

I flinched. I didn't want Michelle to think I'd said anything to Max and Anna about moving in with her, didn't want to come off as a stereotypical U-Haul lesbian. This was the first time I'd spent with Max and Anna since Anna confronted me, and even though they were behaving normally, I felt nervous and hypersensitive.

Michelle didn't even look up from mixing the cornbread. "Oh, Celie's used to cats. My ex-roommate had one." She crooned, "What do you say to the cat, Miss Celie?"

"Heeere, kitty, kitty. Heeere, kitty, kitty," Celie squawked.

We all laughed, and Michelle slipped a sunflower seed into Celie's beak. "She used to drive that damn cat crazy. He couldn't figure out who was calling him to save his life. Here, Celie, you go back to your perch while I open the oven door." She poured the cornbread batter into a sizzling cast-iron skillet and shoved it in the oven. "Why don't we go in the living room where it's comfy? We're still waiting on one guest, and she's workin' on Gay Standard and Colored People's Time."

"Who is she?" I was afraid of meeting one of Michelle's ex-girlfriends.

"She," Michelle announced, "is my secret weapon in the war against Grady Combs."

We settled into the living room. I cuddled up next to Michelle on the overstuffed couch. The living room was filled with thriving plants and photos of friends and heroines. I picked up a picture of two little girls in pigtails, holding hands and grinning broadly for the camera, revealing that they were each missing the same front tooth. "Who's this?" I asked.

"The one on the right is Shawna, my best friend in grade school. The one on the left is me."

"Aww, weren't you cute?" I pinched her face. "And you've still got those chubby wittle cheeks!"

"Y'all are in that sickening lovey-dovey stage, aren't you?" Christopher sighed.

Anna laughed. "Oh, let 'em enjoy it. That's what new love is all about — making single people and old married people sick to their stomachs."

"Sorry," I said, "we'll try to keep the billing and cooing to a minimum."

Christopher shrugged. "Oh, bill and coo to your heart's content. With the luck I'm having, by the time I get another boyfriend, y'all will qualify as old married people, and then we can come visit and make you nauseated."

"Sounds fair to me," Michelle said. There was a light knock on the door. "Ooh, there's my secret weapon now. 'Scuse me, hon," she said, disentangling herself from me.

Michelle opened the door, and in walked a woman so stunningly beautiful that the room fell silent. In her high-heel boots, she had to be over six feet tall. Her skin was the color of toasted almonds, her bone structure impossibly perfect; everything about her was long, lean, and elegant. Until that moment, I had thought that women like her were artificial computer images created by fashion magazines.

"Hey, darlin'," the vision breathed, kissing Michelle on the cheek. Her voice was low and sexy, like Lauren Bacall telling Bogie to whistle. If this high-heeled, high-femme supermodel was the type Michelle usually went for, then what in blue blazes was she doing with short, sloppy me?

Michelle put her arm around the goddess's microscopic waist and announced, "Everybody, this is one of my oldest —"

"Watch it, honey," the woman warned.

"One of my closest friends, Chastity von Trapp."

Wait a minute. That first name — I had heard it somewhere before. My eyes focused on Chastity's black leather miniskirt and knee boots. Of course. That fateful night at Sprocket's with Circe — it had been too dark for me to discern much about her looks, but a tall, black woman had greeted Circe and gestured to me, saying something about "breaking a new one in." My god, what kind of plan for Grady Combs did Michelle have in mind?

Chastity curled up, catlike, in the wicker chair in the corner. Everyone in the room had been rendered mute by her glamour. "Y'all can talk to me, you know," Chastity said, smiling. "I only bite upon request."

Max was still trying to roll her tongue back into her mouth, so I bit. "So how do you and Michelle know each other?"

Chastity smiled, a little moue. "You must be Jess, the jealous girlfriend. Oh, Michelle and I go waaay back, don't we, Chelle?"

Michelle looked down, embarrassed. "You behave yourself, woman. I've got to check the cornbread."

"OK, Aunt Jemima, you go check the cornbread, and when you come back, why don't you bring me a glass of that cheap chardonnay you keep — with one ice cube?"

"Yes, Mistress," Michelle said, rolling her eyes.

"Mmm . . . now those are words I love to hear," Chastity purred. Jealousy was snapping at me like the jaws of a pit bull. Chastity turned her attention back to me. "Your fears are grounded, Jess. Chelle and I were once . . . involved." She hollered into the kitchen. "Hey, Chelle, you got that old picture of me from high school?"

Michelle returned from the kitchen with Chastity's wine and plucked a framed photo off an end table.

Chastity sipped her wine and studied the photo, grinning. "That was me, all right. Lord, look at that nappy little head." She tossed the photo to me. "Here, take a look, jealous girlfriend!"

I glanced down at the picture to see an attractive, smooth-skinned young black man. "Omigod, you're —"

"That's right, sugar. I'm Michelle's ex-boyfriend. We dated in high school." She gave Michelle a sisterly look. "We didn't have a clue, did we, girl?"

"Not a clue."

"Let me see!" Anna shouted, snatching the photo out of my hands. She and Max perused it, while Christopher, unable to contain his excitement, squealed, "Me next! Me next!"

"Wow," Christopher said admiringly, "you were gorgeous."

Chastity pouted. "And now?"

Christopher blushed. "Oh, well, of course, you're beautiful — just not so much my type."

"Well, I'm the type I was meant to be, and that's all that matters." Chastity looked down at her pushed-up cleavage. "Sometimes Mother Nature just needs a little boost."

We ate our soup in the living room while Michelle and Chastity regaled us with tales of their misguided romance. "Of course, by our senior year, we had kind of caught on to the fact that I liked girls, and Charles —"

"Don't say that name, woman!" Chastity wrinkled her nose in disgust. "Sounds like somebody's old uncle."

"And Mr. Charles Trapp, as she was called then, liked boys," Michelle continued. "But we did go to the prom together. I wore a tux —"

"And I wore a sapphire-blue, sequined evening gown. We looked fabulous."

"We were the talk of the prom."

"I can imagine," Max laughed. "So, Chastity, I hope you don't mind my asking this, but have you had an operation . . . I mean, to . . ."

"You mean, do I still have my dick?"

"Well, yeah."

"I take my hormones every day, and I've had my tits done, but in terms of what's below the waist, I've still got what I was born with. I'm saving up for surgery, but I'm not in a big hurry. It's expensive as hell and twice as painful. Besides, even though I'm very much a woman, I'm still kind of attached to my dick." She sipped her wine delicately and added, "Sentimental reasons."

After Michelle cleared the dishes, she changed from charming hostess to no-nonsense strategist. "OK," she said, "I assume you've all been briefed on the Grady Combs situation."

Chastity laughed. "Get a load of little Angela Davis over there. What is this — a meeting of the Lavender Panthers?"

"Don't make fun of me, Chas," Michelle said. "I just want to teach this white boy a lesson."

Miss Celie flapped into the room and landed on Michelle's shoulder, squawking, "Teach the white boy a lesson! Teach the white boy a lesson!"

"That's right," Michelle crooned, producing a sunflower seed from her shirt pocket.

Miss Celie gobbled the seed, whistled appreciatively, and then, apparently hoping for more, added, "Smash white heterosexual male privilege."

"I've never seen a bird with such a raised consciousness," Anna remarked.

"Look," Chastity said, "I'm all for teaching the white boy a lesson. I just don't see why it takes so much planning. Y'all take me to hear White Boy's crappy little band. Jess invites him to sit at our table, I charm his little boxers off, and then I take him back to my apartment for a scene he'll never forget — no matter how hard he tries!"

Chastity's laugh sounded a little too much like Cruella De Ville's for my comfort. "Uh, excuse my naïveté," I said. "But what exactly do you plan to do to Grady when you get him alone?"

"Well, I figure I'll get him in a vulnerable position, and in addition to revealing some of my . . . er, hidden assets, I'll also show him some of the tricks of my trade."

"And what exactly is your trade?"

Chastity smiled at Michelle. "You didn't tell her?" She sipped her chardonnay coyly and looked back at me. "I've got two jobs, actually. During the day, I'm a manicurist." She paused to survey the perfectly lacquered talons on her outstretched hand, then looked back up at me. "At night, I'm a dominatrix."

For better or for worse, Michelle's little plan was beginning to take shape in my mind. "Oh," I said.

"And," Chastity purred, "in case y'all haven't figured it out yet, I'm not planning on doing Mr. Combs's nails."

Chapter 20

The following Friday night we all crammed into Michelle's car, bound for the Executive Lodge's Cadillac Lounge. Chastity looked stunning. Her hair tumbled down her back in a leonine mane, and her figure, perfected through the miracles of modern science, was encased in the Platonic ideal of a black leather dress.

"Now here's the deal," Michelle said, putting the key in the ignition. "Christopher, I was thinking today that maybe you should pretend to be Chastity's date tonight."

"But what's the sense in that?" Chastity said. "I thought my whole job was to let Mr. Combs know I'm available."

"Well, yeah, but I thought the situation might have more dramatic tension if Christopher pretended to be your no-good boyfriend. Maybe he could hit on Anna, and then Grady could start feeling like maybe you deserved a man who'd appreciate you more."

"So tell me, hon," I said, "is this the most elaborate theatrical production you've ever staged?"

Michelle grinned. "With any luck, this will be my masterpiece."

"So I get to play the damsel in distress?" Chastity snickered at the prospect of feigning vulnerability.

"And I get to be the macho asshole." Christopher clapped his hands. "What fun!"

"Just a hint, stud," Max said. "Macho assholes don't generally clap their hands and make swishy little pronouncements like, 'What fun!' "

"Oh, well," he shrugged, "I guess I'll have to work on my belching and farting then."

"Not in this cramped car you won't," Anna said.

The decor of the Cadillac Lounge evoked the nineteen-fifties as seen through the cash-conscious eyes of a contemporary budget motel manager. Reproductions of posters for Elvis, James Dean, and Marilyn Monroe movies hung on walls of flocked red velvet. It was like a cross between a fifties malt shop and an Old West whorehouse.

Except for three or four tables of sozzled-looking white businessmen, the place was deserted. Chastity leaned toward Michelle and stage-whispered, "Do you think we're the first black women to enter this place of our own free will?"

"I'd bet on it."

By the time we sat down and ordered our drinks, Grady and the Diamondtones had started their first set. They were bad — excruciatingly bad, really, doing uninspired covers of Neil Diamond ditties and songs I was surprised anyone remembered well enough to bother to play, like "Brandy (You're a Fine Girl)."

Then the moment of horror came. Grady spotted me in the audience (which wasn't too hard, since the place wasn't exactly packed) and announced, "I'd like to dedicate this next number to a special lady in the audience. Jess Hamlin, this one's for you."

The band then proceeded to play a particularly jerky version of Neil Diamond's "Kentucky Woman," the entirety of which Grady sang looking straight at me. I was mortified, Max and Anna and Christopher were suppressing a giggling fit, and Michelle was ready to scrap her elaborate plan in favor of smashing a beer pitcher over Grady Combs's head. Chastity just patted our hands and smiled. "Patience, girls, patience."

The instant the first set was over, Grady made a beeline for our table. "Jess," he said, grinning like Teddy Roosevelt, "Glad you could make it. How'd you like our little song to you?"

"Well, uh, I hadn't heard that one in a long time, Grady. Here, let me introduce you around. This is my — this is Michelle."

" 'Lo," Michelle grunted. She was a great director, but not a good enough actress to fake friendliness toward a sworn enemy.

"This is Max and Anna, and this is Chris and his girlfriend Chastity."

Chastity rose to her feet and leaned over the table, nearly upsetting the beer pitcher with her breasts. She extended her right hand — to be kissed, not shaken. "Charmed," she purred.

Grady clearly didn't know what to do. He took her hand and patted it as if he might be patting the coon dog he had spoken of a few short days ago. "Yes, ma'am," he said, grinning. "Yes, ma'am." He turned to Christopher. "These pretty ladies sure do brighten up a room, don't they?"

"You got that right, buddy," Christopher replied, leering theatrically at Anna, who bit her lip to keep from laughing.

A syrupy pop ballad came on the jukebox. "Hey, they're playing our song," Christopher said.

Chastity looked at him kittenishly. "Our song, baby?"

"No, doll." He turned to Anna. "Our song." He grabbed Anna by the arm and dragged her to the minuscule dance floor.

Chastity gave a pained sniffle, then looked at Grady with doelike eyes. "Would you care to join us for a drink, Mr. Combs?" She patted Christopher's vacant seat. I glanced over at the dance floor, where Christopher was tripping the light fantastic entirely too gracefully for the macho asshole he was supposedly portraying.

Grady plopped down in Christopher's seat. "I don't mind if I do, but it'll have to be a quick one." He looked Chastity up and down. "That's an awful nice dress."

"Thank you," she said, running a professionally manicured hand down the garment's scandalously

175

short length. "I love leather. I know some people say wearing it's wrong, but me, I don't care much for those animal rights activists. Do you, Mr. Combs?"

Naturally, this got Grady off on a huge tangent about man having dominance over animals and his God-given right to shoot Bambi and eat his still-beating heart if he wanted to, and throughout his ranting, Chastity was staring at him as though he were the most fascinating person who had ever walked the earth.

Before he got up to play the second set, he half whispered, "Do you mind if I give you a piece of advice, Chastity?"

"I would be most interested to hear it," Chastity said seriously.

Grady cast a worried glance at Christopher, who seemed to be under the delusion that Fred Astaire was some kind of macho role model and was dipping Anna so enthusiastically that she nearly bumped her head on the floor. "It seems to me," Grady began, "that you need to find a man who knows how to treat a lady."

Chastity blinked, as though blinking back tears. "I'll take your advice under consideration, Mr. Combs."

"Please ... call me Grady."

Chastity surveyed Grady coolly as he returned to the small platform that served as a stage. "I've got him." She checked her reflection in the mirror across from our table, and spoke to it more than to us. "Of course, I generally like my clients to be better-looking when I'm taking them on a pro bono basis."

Responding to her reluctance, I said, "You can quit now, if you want, Chastity. I can be content the rest of my life knowing that Mr. Family Values over there once lusted in his heart for a preoperative transsexual dominatrix."

"I'm not chickening out," Chastity replied, draining her wine glass. "I can't wait to feel the whip in my hand. It's just all the making-nice bullshit beforehand that I dread."

Christopher and Anna returned to the table, and Anna immediately knocked back the better part of a mug of beer. "Whew, that last tango about did me in! But I must say, Christopher, you do dance divinely."

"A little too divinely for somebody who's supposed to be straight," Michelle muttered. She leaned toward Christopher and Chastity. "Now here's what y'all need to do."

Unfortunately, Grady and the Diamondtones began tuning up (which didn't sound too different from them playing a song), and I didn't hear a word Michelle said.

"Anybody got any requests?" Grady asked his sparse audience.

"How 'bout 'Lola' by the Kinks?" Max hollered.

"Shh, Maxie," Anna whispered.

"I don't believe I know that one," Grady said. "So how 'bout I play a tune I wrote myself? This one goes out to a special lady in the audience. I believe she knows who she is."

The band then tore into a reprehensible little ditty called "Black Mama/White Daddy." I am not a person inclined toward seeing the world in terms of absolutes; however, this song was the absolute epitome of awfulness. It was musically, politically, and morally repulsive — tuneless, racist, and misogynistic. There was literally nothing good, or even fair to middling,

that could be said about it. Though I tried to block
out the lyrics entirely, the song's chorus still
hammered itself into my brain like a steel spike:

> *I know I'm just a white boy, white boy,*
> *But I still wanna be your love toy, love toy —*
> *Come on, black mama, let me be your daddy*
> *   tonight.*

Years later, when the song was over, only Chastity
applauded.

"How can you even pretend to applaud that?"
Michelle hissed. "It's like a love theme for the KKK!"

"Shh, Shh. I know that, girl," Chastity said,
signaling the bartender for another chardonnay. "I
was applauding myself for the sheer genius of what I
plan to do to Grady Combs."

I was beginning to wonder if the second set would
be over by the time I was eligible for an AARP card.
When it finally did end, with a supposedly rockin'
version of "Rock of Ages" to "give everybody out
there something to think about," Grady came sidling
over to our table. The transference of affection was
obviously complete; Grady's goo-goo eyes were
completely focused on Chastity. To my relief, I was
invisible.

"So, uh, what did you think of my song?"

Chastity batted her lashes. "Well, Grady, I —"

"I'll tell you what I thought of your song,"
Christopher burst in, summoning all his testosterone.
"I think you're sniffing around my woman!"

"Well, you certainly don't seem to have much
interest in her."

"Now, now, boys, cockfighting is illegal in the state

of Kentucky," Chastity purred, patting each man on the shoulder. "There's no need to start trouble —"

"As I recall, I wasn't the one who started the trouble," Christopher bellowed like an oversexed bull. I was surprised. He was turning into quite an actor. "Chastity, you were the one who dragged us to this dump of a bar to see this shitty band. Little did I know you had something going with this little homunculus of a singer —"

"Now wait a minute —" Grady began. I was sure he didn't know what a homunculus was, but he seemed to have picked up the fact that it wasn't a compliment.

"Grady, you're a gentleman. You have no place in this argument," Chastity said. "But you, Chris, you and that white-trash slut over there —" She slapped Christopher's face, hard. "Get out! Get your sorry unfaithful ass out of here!"

Christopher clutched his reddened cheek. "Fine. I have better things to do than spend my evenings with a groupie for a third-rate rock band." He grabbed Anna's arm. "Come on, babe, we're going someplace nice."

Chastity made a great show of wiping her eyes. "My goodness, I seem to have talked myself out of an escort. Grady, I'm so sorry you had to see that, and I hate to trouble you more, but could you possibly give me a ride home?"

"I'd be delighted. I'm always happy to help a lady in need."

"Chastity," I said, my voice dripping with sisterly concern, "are you sure you're gonna be all right?"

"Oh, I'm gonna be just fine, with Mr. Combs here taking care of me. You girls go on home."

179

We staggered out of the bar, weak with laughter. Chris was leaning against Michelle's car, holding a handful of ice from the motel ice machine against his face. "You didn't tell me she was going to hit me," he said to Michelle.

"It wasn't in the script," Michelle laughed. "But if that's what she does to you, just imagine what she's gonna do to Grady."

The plan was now in Phase Two. We sped to Chastity's apartment building and parked inconspicuously in the back.

Chastity had told us about the walk-in closet in her bedroom, how its door was equipped with a one-way mirrored window like the kind installed in limousines, so that the person behind it could see out without being seen. Apparently, one of her richer and kinkier clients had paid to have it installed, since he liked to watch sadomasochistic displays while being invisible. Chastity's nickname for him was "the fly on the wall."

We entered the walk-in closet and were surprised to discover that even with the five of us inside, it was not at all cramped.

"Good God," I said, "this place is bigger than my apartment."

"Well, time to get comfortable," Michelle said, wrapping an arm around me. "The show starts soon."

"Ow!" Christopher yelped. "I think I was just violated by a spike-heeled shoe."

"Shh, I hear somebody!" Max whispered.

We heard hushed voices in the living room for a few minutes, then the bedroom door swung open. "A tour of an apartment should always include the bedroom, don't you think, Grady?"

He stumbled a little as she led him into the room. He held a glass of amber liquid, which he was letting slosh around a little more than a sober person would.

"You know, I really liked that song you sang to me. I've always found that musicians are very . . . sensitive. Are you sensitive, Grady?" She let her lips come close to his, but not close enough to touch.

"Well, I, uh . . ." He looked for a place to set his drink. Chastity took the glass from his hand and threw it against the wall, causing an explosion of amber liquid and crystal shards.

What happened in the next few seconds was the most amazing thing I have ever witnessed. Like a trapdoor spider that lies in wait and has half-devoured its unsuspecting prey before it even knows it's been attacked, Chastity pounced on Grady Combs. In what at first passed for a passionate embrace, she slammed him against the closed bedroom door and, in two seconds flat, had his hands bound over his head in the elaborate restraint system attached to the door. In two more seconds his ankles were similarly bound.

Anti-affirmative action, feminist-hating, gay-bashing Grady Combs was trussed up like a calf at the rodeo, panting and shaking with terror and excitement. "I've never done nothing like this before, Chastity," he gasped.

"Don't say a word, Grady. I'll be right back."

She disappeared behind the Oriental screen in the corner and began throwing her discarded clothing over it, causing Grady's eyes to bulge as though they might dart from his head on springs. He sucked his mustache in anticipation.

When Chastity emerged, she was wearing a leather bustier which pushed her bosoms to science-fiction heights, a matching micro-miniskirt that could have been crumpled up to fit in a shot glass, and thigh-high, stiletto-heel black leather boots. "You like what you see, boy?" she spat.

"Yes, ma'am —" he began.

"Good. Now here are the rules. Unless it is absolutely necessary, you do not speak. If you must speak, you address me as Mistress. Do you understand?"

Grady squirmed in his restraints. "Yes, but —"

"Yes, what?"

"Yes, mistress."

"Good." She was pacing the room like a panther. "Now if you do scream, if you yell 'stop' or 'no' or beg for mercy, I won't pay any attention. There's only one word that'll make me stop, and that will be our safety word." She stared into space for a moment, searching for a word that could stay in the forefront of Grady's consciousness. "I think our safety word will be *Nixon*. I figure you can remember that, am I right, slave?"

"Yes, mistress."

She went to the cabinet in the corner, retrieved a pair of black-handled scissors, and proceeded to cut Grady Combs's clothes off his body. When he whimpered, she said, "Be still. I'd hate to cut you."

Soon Grady's Rustler jeans and Members Only jacket and undershirt lay in ribbons on the floor, leaving Grady's paunchy, pasty physique covered only by a pair of wing tips, white tube socks, and boxer shorts printed with small pictures of roosters — a sorry double entendre if ever there was one.

Slowly, methodically, Chastity replaced the scissors in the toy cabinet and selected a small, fierce-looking riding crop. "Now we'll get you whipped into shape, boy," she said, whaling away at him unmercifully. "You white boys need to learn some manners —" *Thwack!* "Some submission —" *Thwack!* "Think you can set the rules for everybody else and still do whatever the hell you want to —" *Thwack!* "You and your white —" *Thwack!* "Male —" *Thwack!* "Privilege —" *Thwack! Thwack!*

Grady only winced and whimpered in response.

Chastity withdrew her whip and smiled. She had a million teeth, all of them brilliantly white. "You're liking this a little, Grady, aren't you?" She glanced down at the region where the roosters dwelled. "I didn't think I was mistaken. You're enjoying yourself quite a bit, aren't you Grady?"

"Yes, mistress," he squeaked.

"For a family values-lovin' bigot, you're a pretty kinky fucker, aren't you, Grady?"

"Yes, mistress." His eyes were downcast, and his voice was barely above a whisper.

"Do you love to serve your mistress, Grady?"

"Yes, mistress."

"Would you do anything for your mistress?"

"Yes, mistress."

"Anything?"

"Yes, mistress."

"Anything on earth?"

"Yes, mistress."

With a whip of her arm, she ripped off her wrap-around miniskirt. "Then suck . . . my . . . dick!" she roared.

Grady stared for a moment at the unexpected appendage, as if he might not recognize what it was. Then his eyes widened, his mouth dropped open, and he began screaming so loudly that anyone in

Kentucky or any neighboring state could hear him, "Nixon! Nixon! Nixon! Untie me! Untie me! Nixon!"

Chastity freed Grady as quickly as she had bound him, and he turned tail and ran, clad only in his boxer shorts, socks, and shoes, and was out the door quicker than you could say *Deep Throat*.

Chastity immediately lost her cool, duchess-of-discipline demeanor and doubled over laughing her raspy, husky guffaw, pausing only to cover her incongruous genitalia. She swung the door open to find the five of us in a giggling heap. She raised her eyebrows in feigned shock. "What are y'all doing in there, having an orgy? Come out of the closet, you perverts!"

Chapter 21

"Heere, kitty, kitty!" Miss Celie called from her cage.

"Mew?" Oscar replied, looking around inquisitively, his tail a quivering question mark, until finally, driven to a record state of feline neurosis, he threw himself at my thrift-store aluminum Christmas tree. He clung desperately to a branch for about two seconds, but it fell off, taking him with it. He arose with great dignity and pussyfooted into the kitchen to sulk.

"Here, kitty, kitty," Miss Celie called again.

Michelle laughed. "This is going well."

Our past couple of dates, we had attempted to get "the kids," as we had jokingly begun to call them, together. We wanted them to get used to each other, since we were moving in together after my lease ran out in the spring.

I rested my head on Michelle's shoulder. "Part of me really wishes I could take you home with me for Christmas, but the rest of me knows it would drive everybody, myself included, absolutely insane."

"Hey, I'd be polite," Michelle said, grinning. "I'd say 'ma'am' and 'sir' and not pick my nose at the dinner table. And what could be a bigger Christmas surprise? 'Mom, Dad, Grandma, Grandpa, I'd like you to meet my black lesbian lover.'"

I laughed and shivered simultaneously, picturing the scene. "Nanny hasn't even got used to black people being on TV yet, let alone in her grand-daughter's bed."

"Yeah, well, I've never taken a girlfriend to meet my family, and I never plan on it. Every Christmas is the same. Mama asks me if I've got a man yet, I say 'No, I'm gay,' and from then on, I'm lucky if I even get asked to pass the potatoes."

I stroked her hair. "Well, you're very brave to be so out to them. I think my parents'll be OK when I tell them, but I want to give them a little more time to get used to me being grown up." I sighed. "I want to give myself a little more time, too."

She kissed me lightly on the forehead. "There's nothing wrong with waiting a while." She glanced at the packages under the tree. "Except when it comes to having Christmas."

"Is that statement to be translated as, 'I want my present'?"

"Loosely, yes."

"OK, just let me see if the cider's ready." I went into the kitchen, fetched two mugs of hot cider, and tossed a treat to Oscar in hopes of soothing his wounded pride.

I sat down beside the tree and handed Michelle a hefty package wrapped in pink foil. "It's not a fruitcake."

She started carefully, sliding her index finger under the seams of the wrapping paper, then muttered, "Aw, fuck it," and tore into it with gusto, until she held the unwrapped book lovingly in her hands. "Audre Lorde."

"I noticed how you have *Zami* and *Sister Outsider* perpetually checked out from the library. This has both of them in the same volume, along with one of her poetry collections."

"Thank you so much. It's so nice to get a gift from somebody who really thought about what I want. I guarantee you, my parents will buy me some ugly-ass sweater, and it won't even be the right size." She picked up a tiny box and handed it to me. "Here, this is for you. The world's smallest fruitcake."

I lifted the lid off and pulled out a small but incredibly detailed silver pendant depicting the Sphinx in profile. It hung on the most delicate of silver chains. "It's beautiful."

"I saw it, and it made me think of that day we met by the Peaslee Sphinx, you know, when we first got together."

"It's perfect. Could you put it on for me?"

I held up my hair and she fastened the clasp, then wrapped her arms around me, hugging me close from behind. I turned to kiss her. She tasted of apples and cinnamon.

Soon we were stretched beneath the aluminum Christmas tree, and she was undressing me the same way she had unwrapped her present — first carefully, then with abandon. Lips locked, arms and legs tangled, we rolled together on the carpet beneath the aluminum tree, the lights from the spinning color wheel turning us all the colors of the rainbow. A mug of cider spilled onto my hair, and a piece of wrapping paper was stuck to my ass, but I didn't care. All that mattered was her mouth on me, her hands on me, in me. As we lay there, laughing ourselves silly from the pleasure, the phrase, "Make the yuletide gay" kept running through my mind.

The next morning, Michelle touched my shoulder. "Baby, you need to wake up. It's almost 11:30."

"Huh? Eleven-thirty?" My heart thudded in my chest. "I was supposed to have left for my parents' over an hour ago."

"I know. Here." She handed me a steaming mug. "Drink this."

Mutely, I obeyed, hoping the caffeine would kick my butt into action.

"I would've got you up earlier, but I just woke up myself. Unlike some people — well, not people, really, but —"

"Huh?" I was still dull-witted from sleep.

"Look over there." Michelle gestured to the corner, where Miss Celie was in her cage asleep, her head tucked under her wing. Oscar was curled up at the base of the cage, also snoozing away. "Here's to unlikely couples," Michelle said, clicking our mugs in a toast.

As much as I wanted to linger on the futon with Michelle, I knew that my mom would blow a gasket if I wasn't home in time for Christmas Eve dinner. If I could get on the road by 12:30, I'd just make it. I jumped in the shower for a quick hosing-off, then threw on a sweater and the ripped jeans that Nanny hated, ensuring that she and I wouldn't want for conversation. As I was throwing socks and underwear into my overnight bag, I noticed the message light flashing on my answering machine. "Hon, do you remember the phone ringing last night?"

Michelle, who had been watching with amusement as I madly rushed about, said, "Vaguely. I was kind of . . . distracted at the time."

"Not as distracted as I was. I didn't even hear it." I turned the volume up on the machine and pushed "play."

"Hey girls, Chastity here. I know y'all are probably too, uh, busy to answer, but I just have to tell somebody this, even if I'm just talking to a machine. When I got home tonight, there was a message on my machine . . . from Grady Combs. He wanted to know if maybe I might call him sometime." The sound of Chastity's laughter filled the room. "You know how those right-wingers are always saying homosexuals recruit straight people? Well, I guess I've recruited me one now!"

Michelle and I took one look at each other and collapsed in laughter. Finally, wiping her eyes,

189

Michelle said, "Well, I thought we were getting even with ol' Grady. I guess we were really doing him a favor."

"Maybe we were doing the world a favor. Maybe Grady will be a better person by virtue of having the crap beaten out of him on a regular basis." I sat for a moment to catch my breath from laughing. "Well, I guess I'll take my overnight bag and the sack of presents to the car. I'll come back for Oscar . . . and for a kiss."

On the way back from the car, I stopped at the mailbox. On the way up the stairs, I started leafing through the envelopes. There was a garish envelope with block letters alerting me that I may have already won ten million dollars, a credit-card offer, a flyer for a pizza joint, and a small envelope with my address handwritten on it. I was opening the second envelope which had been in the first one when I walked into the apartment.

"Mail come?" Michelle asked.

"Mm-hm." I looked at the card inside the envelope and read

Mr. and Mrs. Ray Reed
invite you to witness the marriage of their daughter
Sarah Elizabeth
to
Michael Eric Wilson

"Anything good?" Michelle asked.
"Nope. Just junk mail."

Epilogue

It's fall again. The streets of Old Louisville are packed with tents full of paintings, pottery, and jewelry; the air is rich with the smell of gyros, bratwurst, and barbecue. Max and Anna stop to admire an abstract oil painting and wonder aloud how it would look over their sofa.

"No offense, girls," says Steve, Christopher's new boyfriend, "but my nephew can draw a better picture than that, and he's only two."

"He's so unsophisticated," Christopher says, wrapping his arm around his partner. "If there ain't dogs playing poker in it, it's not art, as far as he's concerned."

"Well, he's cute, though, and that counts for something." Chastity looks toward her date, a handsome young Asian-American man who looks at her with the eyes of a devout worshiper. "Not as cute as this one, perhaps." She smiles wickedly. "But then again, he's probably not as much of a discipline problem."

As we walk past a biergarten set up by the local German restaurant, I do a double take. The woman sitting at the table with the brown-haired neo-hippie — the spiky hair, the leather jacket. She spots me before I gain the confidence to approach her and hollers, "Jess! Get over here!"

"B. J.?" I excuse myself from my friends and motion to Michelle to join me. When we arrive at B. J.'s table, I say, "Since when are you back in town?"

"Aah, I've been back a coupla weeks. I got a bellyful of Cincinnati and came back here and got my old job back. The reason I didn't call you is —" She glances over at her friend. "I met the one dyke in this town I hadn't dated yet. This is Jennifer."

And it is. The very same Jennifer I had disgusted with my crustacean-crunching. B. J. must be back on the rabbit food. I smile at Jennifer, and to my relief, she smiles back. "We've met. As a matter of fact, we had one of the worst dates ever experienced by two humans."

Jennifer laughs. "It was pretty bad. No hard feelings, though?"

"None at all. This is my girlfriend, Michelle. B. J., you may remember her —"

"You're damn right I remember her. I never forget

a beautiful woman." She chucks my shoulder, hard. "Good goin', Jess!"

"Thanks," I say, rubbing my aching shoulder. "Well, give me a call sometime."

"Will do."

"Nothing like being looked at like a slab of meat in a butcher shop window," Michelle mutters as we walk away.

"Don't take it personally. That's just how B. J. is. She just can't look at a beautiful woman without expressing her appreciation."

Michelle looks at me for a long moment, then reaches up to brush back my hair. "I guess I can relate to that."

We join our friends and walk through the fair. I breathe in the delicious air and smile, realizing that, for once, I'm not living in the past or worrying about the future. I'm just walking, carefree among friends, my lover's hand in mine.

A few of the publications of
THE NAIAD PRESS, INC.
P.O. Box 10543   Tallahassee, Florida 32302
Phone (850) 539-5965
Toll-Free Order Number: 1-800-533-1973
Web Site: WWW.NAIADPRESS.COM
Mail orders welcome. Please include 15% postage.
Write or call for our free catalog which also features an
incredible selection of lesbian videos.

LOVE IN THE BALANCE by Marianne K. Martin. 256 pp.
Weighing the costs of love . . .   ISBN 1-56280-199-6 $11.95

PIECE OF MY HEART by Julia Watts. 208 pp. All the
stuff that dreams are made of —   ISBN 1-56280-206-2   11.95

MAKING UP FOR LOST TIME by Karin Kallmaker. 240 pp.
Nobody does it better . . .   ISBN 1-56280-196-1   11.95

GOLD FEVER by Lyn Denison. 224 pp. By author of *Dream
Lover.*   ISBN 1-56280-201-1   11.95

WHEN THE DEAD SPEAK by Therese Szymanski. 224 pp. 2nd
Brett Higgins mystery.   ISBN 1-56280-198-8   11.95

FOURTH DOWN by Kate Calloway. 240 pp. 4th Cassidy James
mystery.   ISBN 1-56280-205-4   11.95

A MOMENT S INDISCRETION by Peggy J. Herring. 176 pp.
There s a fine line between love and lust . . .   ISBN 1-56280-194-5   11.95

CITY LIGHTS/COUNTRY CANDLES by Penny Hayes. 208 pp.
About the women she has known . . .   ISBN 1-56280-195-3   11.95

POSSESSIONS by Kaye Davis. 240 pp. 2nd Maris Middleton
mystery.   ISBN 1-56280-192-9   11.95

A QUESTION OF LOVE by Saxon Bennett. 208 pp. Every
woman is granted one great love.   ISBN 1-56280-205-4   11.95

RHYTHM TIDE by Frankie J. Jones. 160 pp. . . . to desire
passionately and be passionately desired.   ISBN 1-56280-189-9   11.95

PENN VALLEY PHOENIX by Janet McClellan. 208 pp. 2nd
Tru North Mystery.   ISBN 1-56280-200-3   11.95

BY RESERVATION ONLY by Jackie Calhoun. 240 pp. A
chance for true happiness.   ISBN 1-56280-191-0   11.95

OLD BLACK MAGIC by Jaye Maiman. 272 pp. 9th Robin
Miller mystery.   ISBN 1-56280-175-9   11.95

LEGACY OF LOVE by Marianne K. Martin. 240 pp. Women
will do anything for her . . .   ISBN 1-56280-184-8   11.95

LETTING GO by Ann O Leary. 160 pp. Laura, at 39, in love
with 23-year-old Kate.   ISBN 1-56280-183-X   11.95

LADY BE GOOD edited by Barbara Grier and Christine Cassidy.
288 pp. Erotic stories by Naiad Press authors.   ISBN 1-56280-180-5   14.95

CHAIN LETTER by Claire McNab. 288 pp. 9th Carol Ashton
mystery.   ISBN 1-56280-181-3   11.95

NIGHT VISION by Laura Adams. 256 pp. Erotic fantasy romance
by "famous" author.   ISBN 1-56280-182-1   11.95

SEA TO SHINING SEA by Lisa Shapiro. 256 pp. Unable to resist
the raging passion . . .   ISBN 1-56280-177-5   11.95

THIRD DEGREE by Kate Calloway. 224 pp. 3rd Cassidy James
mystery.   ISBN 1-56280-185-6   11.95

WHEN THE DANCING STOPS by Therese Szymanski. 272 pp.
1st Brett Higgins mystery.   ISBN 1-56280-186-4   11.95

PHASES OF THE MOON by Julia Watts. 192 pp. . . . . hungry
for everything life has to offer.   ISBN 1-56280-176-7   11.95

BABY IT S COLD by Jaye Maiman. 256 pp. 5th Robin Miller
mystery.   ISBN 1-56280-156-2   10.95

CLASS REUNION by Linda Hill. 176 pp. The girl from her past . . .
                                              ISBN 1-56280-178-3   11.95

DREAM LOVER by Lyn Denison. 224 pp. A soft, sensuous,
romantic fantasy.   ISBN 1-56280-173-1   11.95

FORTY LOVE by Diana Simmonds. 288 pp. Joyous, heart-
warming romance.   ISBN 1-56280-171-6   11.95

IN THE MOOD by Robbi Sommers. 160 pp. The queen of
erotic tension!   ISBN 1-56280-172-4   11.95

SWIMMING CAT COVE by Lauren Douglas. 192 pp. 2nd
Allison O Neil Mystery.   ISBN 1-56280-168-6   11.95

THE LOVING LESBIAN by Claire McNab and Sharon Gedan.
240 pp. Explore the experiences that make lesbian love unique.
                                              ISBN 1-56280-169-4   14.95

COURTED by Celia Cohen. 160 pp. Sparkling romantic
encounter.   ISBN 1-56280-166-X   11.95

SEASONS OF THE HEART by Jackie Calhoun. 240 pp. Romance
through the years.   ISBN 1-56280-167-8   11.95

K. C. BOMBER by Janet McClellan. 208 pp. 1st Tru North
mystery.   ISBN 1-56280-157-0   11.95

LAST RITES by Tracey Richardson. 192 pp. 1st Stevie Houston
mystery.   ISBN 1-56280-164-3   11.95

EMBRACE IN MOTION by Karin Kallmaker. 256 pp. A whirlwind love affair.   ISBN 1-56280-165-1   11.95

HOT CHECK by Peggy J. Herring. 192 pp. Will workaholic Alice fall for guitarist Ricky?   ISBN 1-56280-163-5   11.95

OLD TIES by Saxon Bennett. 176 pp. Can Cleo surrender to a passionate new love?   ISBN 1-56280-159-7   11.95

LOVE ON THE LINE by Laura DeHart Young. 176 pp. Will Stef win Kay s heart?   ISBN 1-56280-162-7   11.95

DEVIL S LEG CROSSING by Kaye Davis. 192 pp. 1st Maris Middleton mystery.   ISBN 1-56280-158-9   11.95

COSTA BRAVA by Marta Balletbo Coll. 144 pp. Read the book, see the movie!   ISBN 1-56280-153-8   11.95

MEETING MAGDALENE & OTHER STORIES by Marilyn Freeman. 144 pp. Read the book, see the movie!
                                       ISBN 1-56280-170-8   11.95

SECOND FIDDLE by Kate Calloway. 208 pp. P.I. Cassidy James second case.   ISBN 1-56280-169-6   11.95

LAUREL by Isabel Miller. 128 pp. By the author of the beloved *Patience and Sarah.*   ISBN 1-56280-146-5   10.95

LOVE OR MONEY by Jackie Calhoun. 240 pp. The romance of real life.   ISBN 1-56280-147-3   10.95

SMOKE AND MIRRORS by Pat Welch. 224 pp. 5th Helen Black Mystery.   ISBN 1-56280-143-0   10.95

DANCING IN THE DARK edited by Barbara Grier & Christine Cassidy. 272 pp. Erotic love stories by Naiad Press authors.
                                       ISBN 1-56280-144-9   14.95

TIME AND TIME AGAIN by Catherine Ennis. 176 pp. Passionate love affair.   ISBN 1-56280-145-7   10.95

PAXTON COURT by Diane Salvatore. 256 pp. Erotic and wickedly funny contemporary tale about the business of learning to live together.   ISBN 1-56280-114-7   10.95

INNER CIRCLE by Claire McNab. 208 pp. 8th Carol Ashton Mystery.   ISBN 1-56280-135-X   11.95

LESBIAN SEX: AN ORAL HISTORY by Susan Johnson. 240 pp. Need we say more?   ISBN 1-56280-142-2   14.95

WILD THINGS by Karin Kallmaker. 240 pp. By the undisputed mistress of lesbian romance.   ISBN 1-56280-139-2   11.95

THE GIRL NEXT DOOR by Mindy Kaplan. 208 pp. Just what you d expect.   ISBN 1-56280-140-6   11.95

NOW AND THEN by Penny Hayes. 240 pp. Romance on the westward journey.   ISBN 1-56280-121-X   11.95

HEART ON FIRE by Diana Simmonds. 176 pp. The romantic and
erotic rival of *Curious Wine*.   ISBN 1-56280-152-X   11.95

DEATH AT LAVENDER BAY by Lauren Wright Douglas. 208 pp.
1st Allison O Neil Mystery.   ISBN 1-56280-085-X   11.95

YES I SAID YES I WILL by Judith McDaniel. 272 pp. Hot
romance by famous author.   ISBN 1-56280-138-4   11.95

FORBIDDEN FIRES by Margaret C. Anderson. Edited by Mathilda
Hills. 176 pp. Famous author s "unpublished" Lesbian romance.
                                                   ISBN 1-56280-123-6   21.95

SIDE TRACKS by Teresa Stores. 160 pp. Gender-bending
Lesbians on the road.   ISBN 1-56280-122-8   10.95

HOODED MURDER by Annette Van Dyke. 176 pp. 1st Jessie
Batelle Mystery.   ISBN 1-56280-134-1   10.95

WILDWOOD FLOWERS by Julia Watts. 208 pp. Hilarious and
heart-warming tale of true love.   ISBN 1-56280-127-9   10.95

NEVER SAY NEVER by Linda Hill. 224 pp. Rule #1: Never get
involved with . . .   ISBN 1-56280-126-0   11.95

THE SEARCH by Melanie McAllester. 240 pp. Exciting top cop
Tenny Mendoza case.   ISBN 1-56280-150-3   10.95

THE WISH LIST by Saxon Bennett. 192 pp. Romance through
the years.   ISBN 1-56280-125-2   10.95

FIRST IMPRESSIONS by Kate Calloway. 208 pp. P.I. Cassidy
James first case.   ISBN 1-56280-133-3   10.95

OUT OF THE NIGHT by Kris Bruyer. 192 pp. Spine-tingling
thriller.   ISBN 1-56280-120-1   10.95

NORTHERN BLUE by Tracey Richardson. 224 pp. Police recruits
Miki & Miranda — passion in the line of fire. ISBN 1-56280-118-X   10.95

LOVE S HARVEST by Peggy J. Herring. 176 pp. by the author of
Once More With Feeling.   ISBN 1-56280-117-1   10.95

THE COLOR OF WINTER by Lisa Shapiro. 208 pp. Romantic
love beyond your wildest dreams.   ISBN 1-56280-116-3   10.95

FAMILY SECRETS by Laura DeHart Young. 208 pp. Enthralling
romance and suspense.   ISBN 1-56280-119-8   10.95

INLAND PASSAGE by Jane Rule. 288 pp. Tales exploring conven-
tional & unconventional relationships.   ISBN 0-930044-56-8   10.95

DOUBLE BLUFF by Claire McNab. 208 pp. 7th Carol Ashton
Mystery.   ISBN 1-56280-096-5   10.95

BAR GIRLS by Lauran Hoffman. 176 pp. See the movie, read
the book!   ISBN 1-56280-115-5   10.95

THE FIRST TIME EVER edited by Barbara Grier & Christine
Cassidy. 272 pp. Love stories by Naiad Press authors.
                                                   ISBN 1-56280-086-8   14.95

MISS PETTIBONE AND MISS McGRAW by Brenda Weathers. 208 pp. A charming ghostly love story.   ISBN 1-56280-151-1   10.95

CHANGES by Jackie Calhoun. 208 pp. Involved romance and relationships.   ISBN 1-56280-083-3   10.95

FAIR PLAY by Rose Beecham. 256 pp. An Amanda Valentine Mystery.   ISBN 1-56280-081-7   10.95

PAYBACK by Celia Cohen. 176 pp. A gripping thriller of romance, revenge and betrayal.   ISBN 1-56280-084-1   10.95

THE BEACH AFFAIR by Barbara Johnson. 224 pp. Sizzling summer romance/mystery/intrigue.   ISBN 1-56280-090-6   10.95

GETTING THERE by Robbi Sommers. 192 pp. Nobody does it like Robbi!   ISBN 1-56280-099-X   10.95

FINAL CUT by Lisa Haddock. 208 pp. 2nd Carmen Ramirez Mystery.   ISBN 1-56280-088-4   10.95

FLASHPOINT by Katherine V. Forrest. 256 pp. A Lesbian blockbuster!   ISBN 1-56280-079-5   10.95

CLAIRE OF THE MOON by Nicole Conn. Audio Book —Read by Marianne Hyatt.   ISBN 1-56280-113-9   16.95

FOR LOVE AND FOR LIFE: INTIMATE PORTRAITS OF LESBIAN COUPLES by Susan Johnson. 224 pp.   ISBN 1-56280-091-4   14.95

DEVOTION by Mindy Kaplan. 192 pp. See the movie — read the book!   ISBN 1-56280-093-0   10.95

SOMEONE TO WATCH by Jaye Maiman. 272 pp. 4th Robin Miller Mystery.   ISBN 1-56280-095-7   10.95

GREENER THAN GRASS by Jennifer Fulton. 208 pp. A young woman — a stranger in her bed.   ISBN 1-56280-092-2   10.95

TRAVELS WITH DIANA HUNTER by Regine Sands. Erotic lesbian romp. Audio Book (2 cassettes)   ISBN 1-56280-107-4   16.95

CABIN FEVER by Carol Schmidt. 256 pp. Sizzling suspense and passion.   ISBN 1-56280-089-1   10.95

THERE WILL BE NO GOODBYES by Laura DeHart Young. 192 pp. Romantic love, strength, and friendship.   ISBN 1-56280-103-1   10.95

FAULTLINE by Sheila Ortiz Taylor. 144 pp. Joyous comic lesbian novel.   ISBN 1-56280-108-2   9.95

OPEN HOUSE by Pat Welch. 176 pp. 4th Helen Black Mystery.   ISBN 1-56280-102-3   10.95

ONCE MORE WITH FEELING by Peggy J. Herring. 240 pp. Lighthearted, loving romantic adventure.   ISBN 1-56280-089-2   11.95

FOREVER by Evelyn Kennedy. 224 pp. Passionate romance — love overcoming all obstacles.   ISBN 1-56280-094-9   10.95

WHISPERS by Kris Bruyer. 176 pp. Romantic ghost story.
ISBN 1-56280-082-5   10.95

NIGHT SONGS by Penny Mickelbury. 224 pp. 2nd Gianna
Maglione Mystery.   ISBN 1-56280-097-3   10.95

GETTING TO THE POINT by Teresa Stores. 256 pp. Classic
southern Lesbian novel.   ISBN 1-56280-100-7   10.95

PAINTED MOON by Karin Kallmaker. 224 pp. Delicious
Kallmaker romance.   ISBN 1-56280-075-2   11.95

THE MYSTERIOUS NAIAD edited by Katherine V. Forrest &
Barbara Grier. 320 pp. Love stories by Naiad Press authors.
ISBN 1-56280-074-4   14.95

DAUGHTERS OF A CORAL DAWN by Katherine V. Forrest.
240 pp. Tenth Anniversay Edition.   ISBN 1-56280-104-X   11.95

BODY GUARD by Claire McNab. 208 pp. 6th Carol Ashton
Mystery.   ISBN 1-56280-073-6   11.95

CACTUS LOVE by Lee Lynch. 192 pp. Stories by the beloved
storyteller.   ISBN 1-56280-071-X   9.95

SECOND GUESS by Rose Beecham. 216 pp. An Amanda
Valentine Mystery.   ISBN 1-56280-069-8   9.95

A RAGE OF MAIDENS by Lauren Wright Douglas. 240 pp.
6th Caitlin Reece Mystery.   ISBN 1-56280-068-X   10.95

TRIPLE EXPOSURE by Jackie Calhoun. 224 pp. Romantic
drama involving many characters.   ISBN 1-56280-067-1   10.95

PERSONAL ADS by Robbi Sommers. 176 pp. Sizzling short
stories.   ISBN 1-56280-059-0   11.95

CROSSWORDS by Penny Sumner. 256 pp. 2nd Victoria Cross
Mystery.   ISBN 1-56280-064-7   9.95

SWEET CHERRY WINE by Carol Schmidt. 224 pp. A novel of
suspense.   ISBN 1-56280-063-9   9.95

CERTAIN SMILES by Dorothy Tell. 160 pp. Erotic short stories.
ISBN 1-56280-066-3   9.95

EDITED OUT by Lisa Haddock. 224 pp. 1st Carmen Ramirez
Mystery.   ISBN 1-56280-077-9   9.95

WEDNESDAY NIGHTS by Camarin Grae. 288 pp. Sexy
adventure.   ISBN 1-56280-060-4   10.95

SMOKEY O by Celia Cohen. 176 pp. Relationships on the
playing field.   ISBN 1-56280-057-4   9.95

KATHLEEN O DONALD by Penny Hayes. 256 pp. Rose and
Kathleen find each other and employment in 1909 NYC.
ISBN 1-56280-070-1   9.95

STAYING HOME by Elisabeth Nonas. 256 pp. Molly and Alix
want a baby . . . or do they?   ISBN 1-56280-076-0   10.95

TRUE LOVE by Jennifer Fulton. 240 pp. Six lesbians searching
for love in all the "right" places.   ISBN 1-56280-035-3   11.95

KEEPING SECRETS by Penny Mickelbury. 208 pp. 1st Gianna
Maglione Mystery.   ISBN 1-56280-052-3   9.95

THE ROMANTIC NAIAD edited by Katherine V. Forrest &
Barbara Grier. 336 pp. Love stories by Naiad Press authors.
                                                ISBN 1-56280-054-X   14.95

UNDER MY SKIN by Jaye Maiman. 336 pp. 3rd Robin Miller
Mystery.   ISBN 1-56280-049-3.   11.95

CAR POOL by Karin Kallmaker. 272pp. Lesbians on wheels
and then some!   ISBN 1-56280-048-5   10.95

NOT TELLING MOTHER: STORIES FROM A LIFE by Diane
Salvatore. 176 pp. Her 3rd novel.   ISBN 1-56280-044-2   9.95

GOBLIN MARKET by Lauren Wright Douglas. 240pp. 5th Caitlin
Reece Mystery.   ISBN 1-56280-047-7   10.95

FRIENDS AND LOVERS by Jackie Calhoun. 224 pp. Mid-
western Lesbian lives and loves.   ISBN 1-56280-041-8   11.95

BEHIND CLOSED DOORS by Robbi Sommers. 192 pp. Hot,
erotic short stories.   ISBN 1-56280-039-6   11.95

CLAIRE OF THE MOON by Nicole Conn. 192 pp. See the
movie — read the book!   ISBN 1-56280-038-8   11.95

SILENT HEART by Claire McNab. 192 pp. Exotic Lesbian
romance.   ISBN 1-56280-036-1   11.95

THE SPY IN QUESTION by Amanda Kyle Williams. 256 pp.
A Madison McGuire Mystery.   ISBN 1-56280-037-X   9.95

SAVING GRACE by Jennifer Fulton. 240 pp. Adventure and
romantic entanglement.   ISBN 1-56280-051-5   10.95

CURIOUS WINE by Katherine V. Forrest. 176 pp. Tenth Anniver-
sary Edition. The most popular contemporary Lesbian love story.
                                                ISBN 1-56280-053-1   11.95
     Audio Book (2 cassettes)   ISBN 1-56280-105-8   16.95

CHAUTAUQUA by Catherine Ennis. 192 pp. Exciting, romantic
adventure.   ISBN 1-56280-032-9   9.95

A PROPER BURIAL by Pat Welch. 192 pp. 3rd Helen Black
Mystery.   ISBN 1-56280-033-7   9.95

These are just a few of the many Naiad Press titles — we are the oldest and
largest lesbian/feminist publishing company in the world. We also offer an
enormous selection of lesbian video products. Please request a complete
catalog. We offer personal service; we encourage and welcome direct mail
orders from individuals who have limited access to bookstores carrying our
publications.